Nick McDowell has previously published short stories and poetry in magazines, and is currently writing his second novel. He works in publishing and lives in London with his wife and their two daughters.

SCEPTRE

The Wrong Girl

NICK McDOWELL

SCEPTRE

First published in 1995 by Hodder and Stoughton
First published in paperback in 1996 by Hodder and Stoughton
A division of Hodder Headline PLC
A Sceptre Paperback

British Library Cataloguing in Publication Data

McDowell, Nick
  Wrong Girl
  I. Title
  823 [F]

ISBN 0-340-65730-8

Typeset by Hewer Text Composition Services, Edinburgh
Printed and bound in Great Britain by
Cox & Wyman Ltd, Reading, Berkshire

Hodder and Stoughton
A division of Hodder Headline PLC
338 Euston Road
London NW1 3BH

For Sarah, with all my love

I was struck by the beauty of
Roberto Calasso's rendition of the
Pallas and Athena myth in his
The Marriage of Cadmus and Harmony
(Jonathan Cape, 1994) and thank him
for the new light he has shone on their story.

1

Laura Blade

Every evening, an hour before the sun disappears below the western ridge, I tell a story. That's what I'm good at. Sometimes my tales are taken for parables. If you want to hear a message badly enough then that's what you'll hear. Me, I like a good yarn. I am Laura Blade and these are my stories. My stories about me.

There is a palm tree above me. On the wall of a white tower the evening light is tangerine. I am in a circle of friends, passing a bowl of fruit – figs.

It is June, nine months after the events that my story will soon describe.

The wind, which surges insistently down the olive terraces and corrugates the surface of the bay in the daytime, has dropped with the dropping sun.

I have made it a ritual to sit on this terrace, the highest in the hotel grounds, to observe the sunset. Most of the other guests have followed my lead. I like to think they come for the stories as much as the sunset. I imagine myself as a Pied

Piperette who will lead them Gadarene-swine-like over the terrace wall, down the steep scree to mortal injuries on the rocks fifty feet below. Ruptured spleens, white bones pointing through punctured skin. The leader of the pack.

This is tonight's story:

Once upon a time, I took a trip to New York. Or rather my friend Billy asked me along, as you might ask along a roommate you cannot shrug off, out of pity. I can think of better companions – the tone of his invitation implied – but none to whom I am as inconveniently indebted as I am to you. I knew he wanted to ask my twin sister Lizzie with whom he has always been in love. I accepted the invitation knowing that I was a substitute, knowing that had she been available for selection I would have stayed grounded. The number of you'd-better-have-this-then gifts I've received down the years. Starting with Daddy's birthday presents – no, that's unfair. I am like an unfashionable charity – conscience still prompts some broken-down old bibbers to make donations. A clapped-out Oxfam of a girl, slightly discredited but worthy.

But Billy lured me, a premature male menopause in a mac enticing an inner child with bonbons. Have just one, why don't you? Before supper, yes. Come a little closer, then. Come here. Yes, closer still. Yes, there.

If that makes him sound middle-aged, he isn't. If that makes him sound like Daddy, he isn't. We are contemporaries, Billy and I – thirty-something-or-others.

But what had I said to Billy about me and America? I was pretty sure I had told him the New Orleans story (living with two whores and an oil-rig supply worker, the jazz, the Thai sticks, an abortion, a Texan oil-daddy) and quite probably the one that starts isn't-driving-the-breadth-of-America-in-a-T-bird-just-fantastic.

So when he asked me I was insouciance itself. Wouldn't

that be nice. When? Next week? Oh, fine. Great. I'll get a visa.

Had I not been there since the visa waiver scheme began? Of course I had. Forgot all about it (what visa waiver scheme? I wondered, entering familiar deep and murky water).

I pause in the telling and glance to my right, where the manager of the hotel in which we are all residents, a certain Franz Marelli-Kreitznacht, is squirming his plump limbs on an embroidered cushion.

Billy, I continue, was once a criminal. Years ago and at only a modest level of competence. Small-time. Got himself a conviction, nonetheless, for – of all things – shoplifting, and once you have a record or jacket (a term I like, favouring clothes tropes) you have it for life. Name and vitals nestling in an electronic file, waiting to pop up at the push of a button. For ever.

The judge never forgets, the booty is always under your jumper, the stain of finger-printing ink on your feeler-pads perpetual. A trinket here and a trinket there adding up to what the judge called the swag. And what did you do with the swag?

Flushed it, Your Honour. Down the convenience, Your Honour.

You flushed a silver photograph frame?

I didn't take that, Billy said. Not me, Your Honour. (A dozen times, all from good stores; a discerning pair of pickers.)

For his efforts at redistribution Billy received a fine and a sentence held in suspension. Seven, eight years before New York. An upright fellow now. A wiser sinner, sadder and wiser. But a nervous traveller.

On the eve of the New York trip Billy became convinced that somewhere, a computer-link's arc from the

immigration hall at JFK, the details of his exploits and
their attendant punishments were waiting to rebound
upon him.

I'll be an undesirable alien, he thought. They'll throw me
out. Send me home, cast out from the land of opportunity
and cinnamon bagels.

I reassured him as best I could.

Certain that he would never set foot on American soil,
Billy phoned a legal help-line. A sleepy, matter-of-fact
immigration solicitor told him he would be breaking the
law if he omitted any single pertinent fact from the visa
waiver form, then advised him to phone an American
immigration lawyer. We phoned friends who said it would
be fine. What's the worst that can happen? They send you
home. They never check, we were told.

Send me home? Send me home?

Calm down, Billy. Calm down.

Billy found his papers from the court case. After seven
years, he discovered, his conviction had been downgraded.
He didn't exactly *have* a record any more but he was still *on*
record. The thing was stuck to him ontologically even after
he had been released from the fact of it. After a biblical seven
years he had been shrived and partially redeemed.

Does the computer adjust accordingly? he wondered. It
was after midnight. He phoned the American Embassy. No
one would talk to him.

In a moment of inspiration, I phoned the British Embassy
in New York. I explained Billy's dilemma to a chap who told
me that it would probably be all right. I stayed on the line,
begging categorical reassurance.

The vice-consul was consulted. The message came back
in the precise formulations of diplomacy: it would improve
your good standing as a British citizen if you were to
declare yourself at the American Embassy in London before
departure.

Improve your good standing – a ray of hope? No – the

flight leaves before the embassy opens in the morning.
Oh God.

Oh Christ, I thought. I'm going mad. I'll go to Paris.
I hate Americans anyway. Why immigration? Why me?
Why Billy? Why did he have to liberate that silver photo
frame and flush it down the convenience in an attempt to
evade detection? I should be free to jump on a plane with a
light heart. Get an upgrade. Drink drinks. Watch the movie.
Take a pill. Join in with the isn't-America-just-amazing-I-
mean-so-open-and-, like-, can-do conversations. If. If, if.

Billy distracted himself from the panic by considering
how outrageous, how – goodness, I mean – positively
Kafkaesque it was that no one knew who was and who
wasn't in the computer memory and, indeed, who else had
the power to go to the computer tills and withdraw.

He paced the room. He rang the airport: the airline said
forget it, fill in the form, don't tell us stuff we're not
supposed to hear.

He took a shower because all the pacing and sweating had
made him as fragrant as a rotting onion. He shaved his legs
into the bargain (or would have done, had he been a girl
who shaves her legs, as I do). His imagination was vivid
under the jet of water. All the strangers he had talked to
on the phone were squeezed into the stall, jabbering away,
bickering over the shampoo, opinionating, not helping. Pass
the soap, Vice-Consul.

Billy should have been calming my nerves, especially
as my nerves were a result of his. How could he have
constructed such a situation? Unless for the pleasure of
promising me pleasure and then denying it me – denying
the pleasure of another being so much easier – don't I
know it? – than knowing how to take your own and in
taking it give pleasure to another. His face looked like a
clammy hand, stretched flat, given a nose – his rather good
nose, long, with the hint of curve, not beaky but promising
beakiness when he is older and all the girls will want him

still and all the beaky men will be wanting the girls who want them, and I will be left on the shelf to rot (as Mummy might say).

A long walk down the corridors of a hospital where disease and treatment are both abroad, the patients hurried to the operating room by moving pavements. Why do people always wear trainers when they go abroad? Down the ramp, a free copy of the *Daily Mail*. The squeezing of luggage into full overhead lockers. The solicitations of the air nurses. The demonstration of disaster conditions I did not wish to have brought to mind: Code Blue at thirty-five thousand feet.

And, as the plane unstuck itself from the planet, that beautiful I-might-die-in-a-minute-oh-well-here-goes sensation.

I watched Billy trying to meditate on the plane. I picked at his untouched meals. I ordered his drinks and held his hand.

I wished it had been Daddy and not Billy sitting next to me. He loved flying and I loved flying with him. He encouraged my pleasure in flight and I his.

But instead I had the perspiring Billy, smelling staler by the hour, and the threat of a weekend alone in New York without either the man who had invited me or any money with which to shop away his absence. I had not dared use a credit card in weeks. I can never remember my limit and prefer not to use plastic at all than risk seeing it hacked in half by some indignant retailer.

Try to stop blinking, I said to him in the immigration hall. They'll think you're on something.

Five counters and no way of telling what randomness in the movement of the queue would lead us to which counter and thus which immigration officer. They are people, of course, these officials. I hope they had a good lunch. One big woman smiling, broad-faced, coffee-coloured, big-hearted-looking. Be cool, Billy muttered. Which made things worse as Billy would never say anything as nerdy as that unless he felt completely uncool. The phrase let me keep my grip – an absurd little mantra – kept circling in my head to the tune of 'The Grand Old Duke of York'.

'You folks here for a weekend break?' We had the big-heart.

'First time we've left the twins,' I said. 'I'm so excited.'

'Kids. Sometimes you just need to get right away. Where you staying, ma'am?'

Billy juddered beside me, a train passing in a tunnel, rumbling everything. I told her the name of the hotel.

'First time in New York?'

'Yes,' I said. Billy was too gone to notice.

'I don't see any kids in your passport, miss.'

'Identical twins. Katherine and Isabel. Too small for abroad.'

She pulled out a register, a huge binder holding A3 computer sheets. Flicked through to our alphabetical nemesis and lingered there. I was ready to faint.

'I try to get my man to take me away for a weekend' – she looked up at Billy – 'but will he?' Then she slammed the book shut and stamped our passports. 'I could do with a break from the kids myself.'

'Why not sons?' Billy asked as he eyed the carousel for his old sail-bag and my stolen Samsonite.

'Charles. Or Jim, even.'

I wanted a Katherine or an Isabel with me then, Katherine holding one hand, Isabel the other, asking in turn, Mummy, are we in New York now? Mummy, where's the hotel? Where's McDonald's? Is this the FAO Schwartz place?, and so on. But I had only my thoughts for companions, unless you count Billy, who was by now complaining of incipient migraine. The result no doubt of too much excitement in a day. My companionable thoughts said to me: you're in America, no one repatriated you, and you're a mother, to boot.

Katherine and Isabel to take care of, as well as Billy.

Is shoplifting so terrible, so awfully high on the list of cardinals that it should merit exclusion from the land of the free? There's more – or perhaps less – to it than covetousness. It's more like picking your toenails or pulling threads from a jumper. Billy made me promise not to in New York, forcing me to list him alongside other men for whom I have failed to keep promises.

The egg-yellow cab was overpowered. Billy shielded his eyes – from the magnificence of Manhattan or merely the light or both. He was sick to his stomach (see? – all the local turns of phrase). I cradled his head, both windows down. He mumbled about being too hot. It was a cool autumn day, with no hint of the tarmac shimmer in which Nick Carraway had seen sheep on Fifth Avenue. Billy was sick out of the window.

At our midtown hotel I installed him in the darkened bedroom and summoned a doctor.

With my patient attended to, I took a stroll along wide-pavemented Fifth Avenue. I formed the impression that I was wearing goggles, high air streaming under my fuselage.

Do you know about New York's market in air? There is a limit to how high you can build in certain zones. If you want to build beyond the limit, you buy extra height allowances from the owners of buildings that rise to below the decreed limit. Ten feet from Ken Lo, eighty feet from Jerry Hall, until you have accumulated enough of their lowliness to sanction your overreach.

It seems to me to be an equitable system. How much of other people's candour have I had to beg, steal and borrow to boost my powers of invention?

The lowliness of the many can be bought by the few who shall rise above their peers and neighbours. A principle for America.

Just as the system was designed to keep buildings low by

making height expensive, so, I suppose, the high price of invention herds us towards the economy of truth.

I build in air and don't pay my bills.

I flew along the sidewalk, looking for other gliders.

That night, after Billy's Demerol-zombied betrayal, I would dream of a city where dormitories of air had been built from the clear space above low-rise buildings. In my dream I was an entrepreneur of unbuilt top floors. I was latently (but savagely) fucked by a possible Italian with a bow-shaped dick in a potential penthouse high above the city. I constructed hostels out of air for my sorority of gliders and floaters.

Well, I have run on a little. The sun has dropped, unsaluted. In the circle there are shiftings, as guests rearrange stiff limbs. Do I detect a hint of embarrassment in the silence they make over the carpet of percussive cicada sounds? Aren't they used to me by now?

I turn away from the circle and light a cigarette, pretending not to listen out for the things they are saying about me as they take the steps from the terrace down to the dining room.

2 ∫

The next evening at sunset I tell Franz Marelli-Kreitznacht and the guests at the hotel more about my time in New York:

A museum, I tell them, was a safe place to go. Lots to look at and very hard to take anything away. The worst that could happen would be finding that a person would leave with a clutch of unbought postcards. That person might offer the cards to Billy, a gift, a get-well-soon gesture.

From the steps outside the Metropolitan I watched a cluster of Japanese photographing yellow taxis, each other and, in one case, a black-windowed stretch limo burbling at the kerb.

I imagined a special lens with which you might penetrate the mirroring blackness to spy on the shrinking VIPs within. I guessed at the people inside, inventing them in flashes, with each click and wind-on whirr of the camera.

I imagined birds, winged men.

Then I imagined the bodies of two boys (their heads obscured by the angle) and the details of the snake-shaped buckles of their elasticated belts. No heads and no shoes, the latter more frustrating because shoes tell you so much about the wearer – sneakers, loafers, sling-backs, Timberlands (another instance of urban pastoral, please note), and kickers. Kickers kill me – the footwear of the budding child: prepubescent, presexual, inner shoes. Why do they get worn so much by middle-aged men? Shoe-blindness is a terrible affliction.

When the uniformed chauffeur of the photographed limousine actually opened his door he wore orange-flashed trainers with a grey suit.

He released two women and two young boys from the back. Were these mothers and sons? Hal and Hughie, Joel and Jimmy? Nephews, godsons?

The first woman (tartan suit, green-based, elegant, court shoes with too much gold caked to the front, blonde hair scooped in above the shoulder) looked divorced or married to a divorcee. Perhaps the boys were newly acquired stepsons. The second woman wore a long black coat, ankle boots à la mode with sixties heels – was she out of date or was I?

The consonance between the boys I had imagined in the back of the limo and their actual emergence from it drew me to them. I received a small jolt of that nonsensical it-was-meant-to-be feeling, only slightly diminished by the fact that the boys wore regular black belts with pin-and-gate buckles, while my imagination had given them snake-buckled belts.

Is that feeling of connectedness – of wires crossing and things interrelating more tightly than usual – a feature of jet-lag? Or just a result of my crusade against the fragmentary way that things have of falling apart instead of coming together? Answers on a postcard, please.

Anyway, the boys and I were coming together, as I followed the quartet into the museum and waited behind them while the women made enquiries at the information desk in the centre of the booming entrance hall.

I daydreamed about adopting the boys, getting them away from the horrid women. I would teach them about sheep-rearing, herd management, foodstuffs, wool. In the year's gap before university they would go to Australia as jackaroos: I would place them with cousins of my father. They would stay there, fulfilling my father's idea that we should return to his birthplace. I would visit them in New South Wales and discover that they were farming the very fields of my father's childhood, the place from which my grandfather ran his soft-drinks distributorship before Granny took him back to Italy and made a Mediterranean of him, turning John Blade into Gianni. The boys, Joel and Jimmy, would become big wheels in New South Wales, and these women – now exclaiming before a Matisse, whispering at a Pollock – would unparcel their deprivation like a gift.

One boy passed bubblegum to the other. They chewed surreptitiously.

They have something of Billy, these boys. The shape of the eyes (not the colour – blue to Billy's hazel) and in the contour of the head, rather flat at the medulla.

Following the women, I watched them not watching the boys. It was clear that the boys had endured similar disregard before. They knew just how close to an exhibit their busy hands could reach before a commissionaire would rise from his seat by the threshold. They needed reminding that those objects, made by human hands, must not be touched.

Diana, for that is the name I decided to give her, in the tartan with the court shoes and the firmly set blonde hairdo, said to her companion, 'They get it from David. He tells them terrible things. Terrible things I am supposed to have done.'

'And they believe him' – the woman in black appropriated the sentence as if it were really hers – 'because they hardly see him and when they do he lets them do whatever the hell they want.'

Diana wasn't going to leave it at that. It was her sentence and she was going to finish it:

'He'll fight me for those children. Even if he hates them.'

The boys must have heard this but if they had any sense they would let the sounds from Diana's mouth stay sounds and not allow the meaning of her words to form in their ears. Diana turned towards me and I dipped away. The boys moved into another room. I followed.

We are in the section of the museum dedicated to the native art and craft of the Irian Jaya. A long canoe is laid flat in a modern yacht sling. It contains hand-made symbols of sacrifice, the trappings of a cult I don't know about, swords, lances, masks, wooden carved animals, narrow women. Stretched to the high ceiling are totem poles – more animals, symbols, ball-breasted women. This section is at the edge of the museum where it gives on to the park. There is a tall glass wall sloping in from floor to ceiling. A fine black gauze is stretched close to the glass to filter the light. Looking out, the park is twilit and monochrome. I recognise it as the way parks look in dreams – the colour washed out of the trees, the grass a gentle grey.

The boys are running their hands along the canoe, feeling the bumps in the wood, staring out of the wall-window at the indistinct park in which they would much rather be.

These are my sons. My new twins. Let Billy arrive with the softball and we will run out into the park together.

Yes, let them be my sons, these disregarded boys. Billy will throw the ball for the boys. Joel, who is faster, will sometimes let Jimmy get to the ball before him, because Billy and I will have taught our sons to love one another. Daddy will be on a bench, watching the game. Billy, of whom Daddy continues to disapprove (the idea of just how much he would disapprove of Billy almost brings Daddy back to life), throws the ball so that the boys are forced to run close to Daddy to collect it. He reaches out his hands to touch them as they pass, but they duck and slide past him, an old man who wants to slow them down, who makes them stay at table after they have finished eating. I have the picnic basket. Billy has brought a six-pack. We settle on the grass around Daddy's bench. Luncheon *sur l'herbe*. One day. Some day.

I like this part of the museum with its big black screen on to which I can project my new all-American family. The boys like it too. They are laughing at something, standing beside the window now, on the other side of the long canoe, pointing at something. The guard, a squat Hispanic woman, moves across to them, not to chide but to see what it is that makes them laugh.

On the other side of the glass wall a man stands peering in at us, a fan of the Irian Jaya perhaps, an enthusiast who has been banned for some excess of devotion. No, he is not trying to look in. He raises a pair of scissors, blades open, holding the scissors up and to one side.

There is a moment when I am certain that he will plunge the scissors down into the side of his neck. I see the blood bursting on to the glass, his frame keeling – totem pole to canoe – the blood a fading fountain, lapping against the foot of the glass wall. On an instinct I reach forward to shield the boys but stay my hands just before touching their shoulders. The man stares at us, his audience. The boys are just in front of me, their noses almost touching the glass, only inches (and glass) between them and the scissors. I let my hands settle very lightly on their little shoulders. Neither squirms under my hands.

The scissors swoop down and snatch a curl of hair from the side of the man's head. He catches the hair in a baseball cap which he holds inverted in his free hand.

Others are gathering behind us, the Irian Jaya forgotten, as we watch this most intimate of things. A man cutting his hair in the park. Tears come to my eyes. I can't help myself.

'White trash,' someone says behind me.

It is like watching a young girl touching the first swellings of her breasts, shy and preoccupied, watching her while knowing what she does not know: that her father and his beery friend are watching her through the window.

Our window on to the park is his mirror. We are drinking in his solitude, thirsty for his peaceable aloneness. I like the deliberate way he crops one lock and then another, choosing, planning, running a comb through his hair, cleaning out the comb into his inverted baseball cap.

'Hey,' I shout.

'Hey,' the boys echo me. 'Hey – Mr Man. Hey – Mr Haircut.'

He cannot hear us. He might as well be a prisonner observed through the eyehole in a cell door. We chew on his solitude, the flesh so sweet we cannot quit the carcass. We are jackals, hyenas laughing at our lunch.

His hands whirl about his skull with a lovely aerial elegance as though his arms might double as wings. He feels his beard, pondering its thickness and shape.

We are a crowd now. My hands rest on the narrow shoulders of Diana's boys. The women may be in the crush of people behind me.

I fancy I can see Daddy, out in the park, slumped on the bench, wishing we would run to him. Lizzie, my twin sister (or is it me? – we're impossible to tell apart) on Daddy's lap.

'Come on boys,' I say. 'Let's go get ice-cream.' Their bodies turn under my steering hands.

There is no tartan Diana to stop us, the boys running ahead, knowing their way to the café.

I am trying to remember where the Irian Jaya are, as if recalling that will somehow make the rest of it all right – what we have done to Mr Haircut, out there in the birdsong with dew on his trouser-leg communing with the urban pastoral; and whatever it is that I am doing, taking these boys for ice-cream.

Striding through the sculpture halls, keeping the boys in

my sights, I feel protective and important. I must not let my charges fall into the wrong hands. After the Samsonite suitcase and the silver photo frame, why not twins? Why the hell not a pair of sons?

Joel and Jimmy (I wonder what their real names are?) stand at the entrance to the café. As I join them, a waiter comes towards us and indicates a table from which the last clients' buns and espressos have not yet been cleared.

We sit. The waiters wear white jackets buttoned to the neck which spooks me but I cannot remember why.

'When did you start?' Joel asks.

'You think you're gonna stay with us?' Jimmy says. 'You realise how mean our mom is?'

'Where's the ice-cream?'

'She gonna pay you? How much is she gonna pay you?'

'Quit with the questions,' say I. 'Vanilla or chocolate?' They think I am a servant.

'Banana boat.'

'Hey. English.' Joel pours salt on to the table. 'Pretty cute.'

'There will be no ice-cream if you talk like that.' Christ, I sound like my mother.

The banana boats arrive before the sensation of being my mother departs. I force myself to remain silent while the boys spread ice-cream and mashed banana on the table, on themselves, picking off pieces of chocolate flake with their fingers, smearing it around their mouths.

Jimmy starts to pick his nose. He makes a chocolate rim around each nostril.

'Children are ghastly, darling,' my mother once said to me. 'They don't mean to be. They just are. Messy, selfish and terribly greedy. Characteristics I find awfully hard to admire in anyone. You have to have the presence of mind to train it out of them. To teach them manners, restraint, teach them how to behave.'

Mummy looked up at me to solicit a reply. My expression helped her hear what she had said. She sighed – a sigh potent with sadness and disapproval – and continued. 'You love them, of course. Love them like nothing else. You can't help it – I mean you wouldn't want to help it even if you could, would you? You love them dreadfully, Lorry.'

Please don't call me Lorry.

And if you think I haven't got the bottle for the next bit, stay tuned. I imagine Billy, watching me on the security video, saying to himself, no, she won't, she can't. Then he'll remember how it was me who walked out of Harrods that day with the provisions for the dinner party under my coat. He'll think, Jesus, she's going to. She can, she will. Any minute now.

The table is cream formica, with a narrow hardwood surround. Chocolate in streaks, like dried blood at a crime scene. On their hands, their dark blue jumpers, some on the cuff of my white shirt.

They are whispering in American.

I mean no harm. I mean no fucking harm, all right? So just let it go.

Leave me be. Let me get on with being with my kids, OK? And don't you dare, don't ever think that you can lay a hand on my children.

I'll squeeze until your face turns blue.

The chocolate boys are finished now.

The waiter hovers.

'More,' I say. 'You want more, don't you?'

'Yeah.'

I stare them down, demanding the word of them. Back with Mummy and her greedy-little-monsters approach to child-raising.

'You want that we should say please?'

'Yeah. Please, Miss whoever-you-are.'

'More ice-cream for my twins, please, waiter. More ice-cream all round.'

'Who said we were twins?' asks the boy whom I have designated Joel.

What on earth, beyond ice-cream, do they want of me? Such sweet, such sweet-toothed boys. Their sweet warm hair and grubby hands. Chocolatey fingers and lips and nostrils.

The question hangs in the air. 'Well, aren't you?'

These twins of mine, these sons.

You will be so proud of your sons, Billy. So pleased with me for the way I have looked after them. You will say to our friends – or rather to your friends, who by association sometimes become mine too – she is a wonderful mother, a very natural sort of mother.

The boys want for nothing. Never alone unless they want to be, always up to some wonderful game which Laura has invented for them.

They run into the house – from the farmyard, you see, the farmyard in which they have their own ducks, pigs, goats, chickens, the Welsh farmyard – and fling their arms around her and she wipes the soap-suds from her still-soft hands and says:

'Who are the best-loved boys in the world?'

Billy, the proud husband and father.

He is like one of those sycamore seed-pods. We used to call them helicopters at school. A pill of seed with an aerial fin or solo wing, gyrating and fluttering, down, down, down.

As Billy breaks open on the pavement, six floors below the hotel window, the boys crawl out of the seed-pill, fully formed but very, very small. Like Helen from the swan's egg.

The booming clatter of footfalls echoing in the museum reminds me that Tartan Diana, even allowing for the most extreme degree of parental negligence, will be clicking about in her gold-caked shoes, clucking about in search of the boys.

I think I will be that sycamore seed-pill, thank you very much, with the broken propeller. Going round and round, dropping gently to earth, to be trodden underfoot, crushed open, to multiply, to disseminate.

There will be a lot of me about. I'll be a handful. Billy can search out his own damned analogies. He can be a bramble patch or a geranium – he has a suburban fondness for the geranium.

I pay the waiter for the flotilla of banana boats. He up-ends the saucer so that the change slides straight into a kangaroo pocket at the front of his white tunic.

'Eat as fast as you can. As fast as can be. The wolf is coming to get us, to get us, and we must run away before he arrives. But don't leave any ice-cream or he will know we were here.'

'No wolves in Manhattan, Miss whoever-you-are.'

'You got foxes,' Joel says. 'Neat foxes. Garbage-eating.'

'Ice-cream-eating?' I ask.

'Could be,' says Jimmy. 'Where's Mom?'

Jimmy is the leader, the dominating influence and the protector. Joel is probably the thinker, but right now his brain is being gobbled up by ice-cream, numbed by the chill of it.

'Your mother likes to look at pictures. We must leave her to it. It will elevate her spirit. Lift her up.'

'Mom's pretty high all the time.' Joel spoons a wodge of banana mush into his face.

'Pills for getting up and pills for chilling out. Pills for hanging with friends and crashing pills.' Jimmy has stopped eating.

'And do you borrow Mommy's pills?'

'Would we do that?' Joel grins a mouthful at me.

'I think I would like some pills now, if you have any.' Something is wrong here. Clearly wrong. It is the afternoon of my first day in New York. In London it is bedtime. I feel my skin stretched over the distance, my spirit panting to keep up. So – this is jet-lag.

'Your mother has asked me to take you home while she finishes looking at the pictures.'

'After the Met we go to the park,' Jimmy says. 'Always.'

'The park, then.'

Romulus Joel and Remus Jim head out of the café in front of me, two beacons lighting my way. No wolves in Manhattan, huh?

I could smell the toxic whiff rising from my groin, threatening to choke me, the rich fumes bedizzying. The same musk of excitement as when I lifted a whole side of smoked salmon from Harrods, the fish flopping against my thigh under a long skirt; the smell of the smoked fish and the odour of my simmering fear. This rising sensation in my groin as if I might levitate and glide a centimetre or two from the ground on a cushion of exhilarated terror.

I remember the same promise of lift-off once at school – my sister Lizzie and I were nine – when another girl was accused of stealing Matron's tampons. Lizzie and I had buried them in a wood in the school grounds for future experimentation. I settled my gaze upon Lizzie, locked her with my eyes, forbidding her to speak, rising from the ground, angelically possessed, a stone-faced, unsuspected thief, quashing my accomplice sister's compulsion to confess. What a sweet sensation it was, even though someone else sneaked on us in the end and we had to write to Mummy and Daddy (which, of course, entailed two separate letters) explaining what we had done and why – Lizzie wrote that she wished to 'practise the art of feminine hygiene in preparation for her maturity', a phrase given her by the head girl who had a crush on her. I wrote that someone else had stolen the tampons and we had been blamed, which seemed to me, at the time, to be true. Mummy and Daddy never challenged us on the disparate versions, which means that either one of them didn't read one of the letters (or even both of them read neither of the letters) or that they communicated so little, even then, that the business of their daughters' misdeeds at school did not become a subject of conversation. Either way, for me it was a triumph of the will, over Lizzie, the teachers, my parents, Matron and her arts of feminine hygiene.

The adrenalin gush on top of jet-lag leadens my limbs, the heaviness combining strangely with the floaty gliding of my feet over the marble floors. Only the guiding beacons of the boys ahead keep me from swooning.

I imagine my crumpled self on the floor, a heap of limbs and clothes, the boys coming back for me, bending over me, Joel applying the kiss of life while Jimmy palpitates my heart with his sticky little hands.

At the main doors of the museum, in the confluence of eager arrival and spent departure, I badly want to run, to spin my legs in the air like a cartoon criminal in a face-mask and spurt for safety.

There is always this moment where the desire to abandon control, to capsize the artistry of the operation, threatens to overwhelm me. Here are the familiar commissionaires, opening doors for old ladies and the emprammed. And the bored security guards, counting off the minutes until the next cigarette break. It is best to wait for some distraction before shimmying past these mastodons. The times I have almost kicked down the final hurdle on the very threshold of victory, the urge to spring like a sneeze building at the back of my nose.

I've had it with this present tense (and with the present, pretty much). I'm not sure it makes anything or anyone more present. A tense cannot bring things back, nor can it – more's the pity – make anything go away. It can only bring things into being which were never there in the first place, like the transmuted Daddy and the reconstituted Lizzie of whom I have more to tell.

So I shall call the irredeemable past – which slips daily further from our grasp (as someone once sentimentally wrote) – irredeemable, and give it an appropriate tense. Not through any outmoded respect for decorum, but because I wish to put a distance between us (you and me, dear friends) and what happens – happened – next.

At the main doors of the museum I stood between the boys, took one hand of each and descended the steps with my double cargo, my twin familiars.

The black limousines had multiplied along Fifth Avenue. It was impossible to tell which of the dozen that now ribboned the kerb belonged to Tartan Diana. The day was colder, the autumnal glow of the early afternoon transformed to a grey flatness. How truly the year had given up on itself, even in the Big, upbeat Apple. Some of the chauffeurs stood on the pavement, men who had been squeezed or slotted into their uniforms as into life-circumstances which they had not sought, men who had hoped for better than this. Hair curling over collars at the back, confetti of dandruff on strapped and buttoned shoulders, suit pants pushed down by swollen bellies at the front, sliding off flat buttocks at the back.

They shifted on the sidewalk, hating to be still. I recognised Diana's by the orange flashes on his trainers. Would he care what happened to the boys? Was guardianship included in his duties?

I was planning what I would give them for supper when Jimmy shouted 'NOW!' and the two of them yanked their hands from my grasp. They ran down the steps, racing across the pigeon-strewn demi-piazza with me in hot pursuit. I ran straight into the chauffeur, who grabbed my arm. The boys were holding on to his legs.

I knew I should try to run – anywhere. But it is one of my rules never to run. To run is to admit guilt in advance of accusation: a poor use of moral credit.

'RAPE!!'

The chauffeur's face froze into a look of feral concentration. He'd had something to do with that big word, either as an -ist or an -ee. I felt his grip on my arm loosen; but then he clenched again as he tried to work out the story between me and the boys. I was captivated as much by the reflection of intellectual strain in the musculature of his face as by his meaty hand around my arm.

'RAPE!'

One more shout and he would let go of me. The boys were blabbering some tall story about ice-cream and kidnap. People around us were frozen in place, wanting to intervene, not wanting to get hurt, thinking about being sued, trying to see who was the victim.

'—gave us extra ice-cream.'

'—Mom's pills, I mean maybe a dope fiend.'

The chauffeur was eyeing me with a settled look of disgust.

'—where the fuck, excuse me, are those goddamned kids oh jesus this is New York don't you understand I mean Arabs white-slavery crack and pimps with that whole snuff movie thing and this will definitely fuck right up – excuse me – the alimony if David ever gets to hear do you absolutely promise jesus you can't trust anybody not to tell anything to anyone else in this crazy town even if—'

Coming down the steps towards us, Diana in full flood.

A slow moment in which the greedy interest of the onlookers swelled and swirled and eddied around us – the chauffeur clutched by boys, clutching me, trying to rape me, Diana steaming towards us, her heels in tickertape overdrive, the friend with her hands in her hair and an oh-my-god look on her face. Not long and the Japanese would start snapping – I saw photographs of me in an evidentiary baggy being handed up to the judge by a clerk in a brown suit and knitted puce tie: exhibit A.

Fuck it, excuse me, Diana, I hate to run.

'RAPE!' I yanked back my arm. Boys' hands held me like ivy holds stone, the hands torn off my skirt as I ran straight into the Fifth Avenue traffic, wishing for wings with which to skip, flex and swoop up above my pursuers.

No sons for Billy to play softball with. No nephews for Lizzie to choose ties for. No grandchildren for Daddy not to settle trust funds upon.

When someone tries to rape you, you run if you can and run I did. Twenty-seven – or was it twenty-eight blocks? – back to the hotel.

I was told by a psychiatrist – I don't recall which one; they have about as much character for me as coconuts in a fairground – that shoplifting has nothing to do with acquisition or possession and everything to do with repossession, with reclaiming things lost or mislaid.

Samuel, I think it was. Yes, Samuel, the sensitive shrink. He cares, he invites you to share your feelings. He rubs the sides of his nose. He wore Armani specs, tight-to-the skull curly hair and moleskin slippers which suited his bedside manner. Or couchside, rather. My high command had been carrying out an orderly retreat which had worn the enemy down, left him vibrating with frustration at the end of each session. He would say, self-piteously and as if he were the client, 'We aren't getting very far, are we?', and my parting shot would be, 'Where are we trying to go?' It was dull for me but duller for him. You might say that I was helping Sam to get in touch with some really fundamental feelings. He should have been paying me.

His consulting rooms were near Waterloo Station and after one of the sessions I hopped on the train that Lizzie and I used to take when we went to see Daddy at the weekends, went back to the house and just looked at it and thought about Daddy. I lifted a few things from a shop near the station – silly things: a packet of Polos and some envelopes – and left them by the gate to the house.

A sort of votive offering idea. I became the little girl who had bought a present for her father. Whatever. Anyway.

As I ran down Fifth Avenue, assuming pursuit but not looking back for it, I thought about Samuel – why Samuel? – and I became Samuel because he was fit and used to run on the track at Battersea Park (I followed him there once). I reckoned that being Samuel would make me go faster.

I cannot help this surge towards otherness, into histories – careening down back streets in reverse gear, eyes on the mirror – which aren't mine even if they once might have been. Don't you find it tempting to melt into other people, to let yourself thoroughly become them? Practise their mannerisms, borrow their shoes? No? To colonise their past, to beg, steal, borrow from them?

Near the hotel, when I was very much out of breath, waiting to dart into traffic, I thought: I am a tube of toothpaste, crusted and dried at the top, blocked except for the tiniest worm of peppermint goo that a man can sometimes squeeze from me.

A stone, I said to myself (none of this seemed at all odd at the time) as I entered the hotel lobby, is a form of silence and vice versa. The porter swung the door back for me with really quite perfect timing and I wooshed into the lobby, heaving for air, trying my best to seem composed and tourist-like.

Speech is vegetable, silence mineral, love is animal, urban noise – traffic jangles, radio spluttering – is, as we know, white.

I wanted to ask the porter about this but he turned to help someone with their bags.

'Did you get my prescription, Lorry?' Billy, lying on the bed, looked green.

'Wouldn't give it me on my ID.' I had forgotten about his prescription.

'Buy anything?'

'Twins.'

'Dolls?'

'Yes, dolls.'

Billy looked seedy and cross. The room was too small for all of me and little him on the bed. I elevated above the streets of Manhattan – dolls babbling and squeaking, a crowd of dolls squelching speech like animals tortured into anthropomorphism, singing a chorus in a Disney animation.

And my head swung round to the past, in the hateful way it does, to that picture of the gate to Daddy's house in the country and the gate will not open and Daddy and Margaret (my nanny-turned-stepmother . . . don't try it, girls, it backfires) with her sad smile because the gate will not open and everyone has to go now. We have to go.

Daddy behind Margaret touching Margaret, lifting one hand from Margaret to wave to us. Goodbye, Bet, good-bye, Lorry.

'These hips of mine.' I swung back to Billy. 'Are they child-bearing?' I moved closer and he sat up on one elbow, his cheek against my belly, trying to work out an answer. I wish he would say the first thing that comes into his head, like I do. Billy looked for the right answer in his reflection in the TV screen. Then he picked up the phone and arranged for the bell-hop to fetch his drugs from the pharmacy.

'Women aren't made to have babies any more, they're made to be dressed. You look great.'

I had expected better, but what did I expect? I had been thinking of Margaret and how maternal she was (much more so, frankly, than Mummy) and how I wanted to look, to be, maternal – kind of milky and rounded and wholesome and hug-giving.

'You don't think we're made like this, do you?'

'I've got a headache. Tell me what you want me to say and I'll say it.'

'I might as well talk to myself.' It hit me then – the

knowledge that I had always been talking to someone else, never to the person whom I appeared to be addressing, talking to that which was absent.

I wanted Lizzie there. Why couldn't she have come too? Billy would have liked it.

Lizzie and I are hard to tell apart and it was out of mutual frustration with our interchangeability that we started to do things with our hair and our weight to try to become distinct from one another. Can you imagine how dull it must have been to be confused with someone else all the time?

'Lizzie?'

'No, Mummy, it's Laura.'

'Oh, dear Laura,' which she made sound like 'Oh dear' with Laura tacked on. As often as not Lizzie and I didn't bother to correct people. We rapidly discovered how much could be gained and risked by letting people suppose that they were talking to Laura when actually it was Lizzie listening or vice versa. And not just with talking and listening.

'How do you know I'm not Lizzie?' I said to Billy.

'Don't be a cunt, Laura.'

I love that word. Loved Billy saying that word, always the trigger word at the point when he decided to stop being whatever it was he was pretending to be for me.

'Do you like my cunt?' I wanted him to go on, get worse, be foul to me. Nuzzle his face against it. 'Does it clutch you hard enough?' But he turned away from me, his hands at his neck. I knew he was thinking, if only I could get her to massage my neck.

After all that ice-cream, all that patience. I had been good to them, hadn't I? And what did I get in return? A chauffeur manhandling me. A din of accusation.

'Well – does it?'

'Yes.' Said with that absurd, throaty, throttled sound that men make when their tassels begin to stiffen.

'You like it, don't you. Say you like it.' (Was he pretending this as well?) 'You can't leave it alone, can you?'

'No. I can't leave it alone.' He turned his headachy little face towards me.

He can't leave it alone. Oh, wake up, Billy. Wake up to what girls do when they can't have what they want because they don't know what they want because no one ever asked them what they wanted, no one ever bothered to ask.

'But you'd rather it was Lizzie, wouldn't you? Even if half the time you can't tell the difference between us. Rather her than me.'

'Not this.' He drew back from me. 'Not now.'

'You hate me knowing her thoughts, but think of the fun you could have. Both of us – serially, multiply, acrobatically, in a ditch, a sewer, in a theme park. Where the fuck – excuse me, Diana – but where the fuck is your imagination?'

'I can't do this.' Sitting up on the bed, rubbing his eyes, holding his head in his hands. There was a knock on the door. The bell-hop with Billy's painkillers. He went into the bathroom with the pharmacy bag, muttering.

As I was saying about Manhattan, there is this alternative island, made of all the air above the low-rise buildings, an atmosphere holding the possible buildings in which my gliders dwell. Hangars, sheds of hope.

The wind buffets, we circle above the metropolis, in our rented airspace, peering down. Vultures above a desert road, our patience sombre, relentless, waiting for death. What would it be like to always be thirsty? To have drunk and yet always remain thirsty? Try to imagine that.

There is also an alternative Billy with pectorals, dorsal fin, tail, full antennae. The confidence of a bluejaw and disregarded hair. A soaring Billy, kept in storage.

I struggled against nursing him.

'When I was modelling—'

'You were never a model,' he said.

'When Lizzie and I modelled, as children. Daddy put us

in for this child fashion thing. Matching sisters sporting matching clothes. Lots of tartan.'

'It never happened.' He was behind me. I stood at the window, wanting to be gone. 'You never did that.'

'They put make-up on us. We were five. Lizzie said, how will they make us up? What will they make us into? Who made us up before this? What are we when we haven't yet been made up? Can we be unmade up?

'I said to her – my mean streak thickening (I had a terrible stomach ache) – if you aren't made up then you aren't there at all. If there's no one to make you up then you just aren't there at all.

'She started crying – imagining herself as a vacuum, an absence. She wanted Mummy, she said. But I knew that she wanted a daddy who would not have landed us in this situation where we had become a photographer's toys for a day.'

Billy channel-switched with the sound off, pretending not to listen to me. I lay down beside him.

'Why can't you just be glad it's me?' I said. 'Instead of wishing I was someone else and you were somewhere else with her?'

'Do you realise how pathetic you sound?'

'But it's true,' I said.

'How can a question be true?'

'She's not such an angel, you know.'

'Wasn't she?'

'When are you going to give me something that you don't take away at the same time?'

'You're impossible to give to,' Billy said. 'You throw presents back at the giver without unwrapping them.'

He turned away from me.

'Tell me a story,' I said. 'You can manage that, at least.'

'You're the storyteller.'

'What's that supposed to mean?'

'Whatever.'

'You're pathetic,' I said to him. 'It's a wonder you can dress yourself in the mornings.'

Nothing more from Billy. Pretending to be asleep.

'I know what we'll do – I'll tell you a story Daddy used to tell to me and Lizzie when we were little. Then you can imagine Lizzie here with us, listening to the story. You'll miss her less and be nicer to me. Won't you? Please?'

I listened to his breathing which he was trying to make regular in a further attempt to convince me that he was asleep. I knew he was listening and this is the story I told him:

New inscriptions, discovered in a burial ground some miles from the site of Babylon by the noted classical archaeologist Carl-Heinz Blatter, imply that the Hanging Gardens – one of the Wonders of the Ancient World – were much larger than the previously available evidence had suggested.

What is more, they did not hang. From Diodorus Siculus onwards, the ancient historians were misled, perhaps by a Babylonian wiliness in the covering of tracks. Perhaps because the true purpose of the Hanging Gardens – which my story will reveal to you – casts a shadow over the myth of Icarus, upon which the Greeks and their successors depended for a set of ideas about the consequences of ambition and excess.

Herodotus writes that the Hanging Gardens were built to appease the homesickness of a princess who missed the landscape of her childhood. She had been raised in the Median hills, to the north-east of Babylonia.

You have to imagine (as Daddy used to command) building a hill four times the size of the Athens Hilton. That is what Nebuchadnezzar ordered to gain the happiness of his bride. A wedding present on a very big scale indeed. As implausible, as magnificent, as Manhattan.

They built the hill out of muck and bound it together with saplings and shrubs. Irrigated it without the help of electricity, using a pulley system driven by the force of the Euphrates dragging buckets through the current and up the hill.

The inscriptions imply that by comparison with the Babylon earthworks, the pyramids were but a passing whim, a folly, an architectural spasm. While the Egyptians were building in preparation for death, the Hanging Gardens proposed a passion in defiance of death, taking a million slaves a decade to build at the cost of two hundred thousand lives. Who is to say which was the mightier gesture? You have to imagine those verdant slopes rising, like Lazarus, from the throbbing desert.

You have to place yourself in the sandals of a trader, leading his caravanserai across the plain to Babylon. You can see birds in the distance. You are still a day's walk from the Ishtar gate. Birds wheeling, soaring, playing on the draughts of hot air streaming up the hillside. Your men are tired. They need new sandals. Tonight you will water your animals and your feet at the banks of the Euphrates. Tomorrow you will trade. You watch the birds burst out of the hillside into the seared blue. It is as if a catapult is launching them into the air.

After noon, when you are closer to the city, you see not birds but – goodness me – men hanging from giant kites made of stretched animal skin. Circling upwards on the currents, corkscrewing towards the sun and gliding out to land in the the flat vastness below.

These are the *crème de la crème* of Babylonia, the polo players of the period, members of the exclusive Babylon Flying Club, patronised by the Median princess. Carl-Heinz Blatter surmises that the Median princess brought with her not a longing for home but for flight. Or rather, it was flight which made her long for home. Once the hill had been constructed and her instructor seconded from his duties in Media, Princess Amyitis became an uncomplaining wife to Nebuchadnezzar and bore him many a child.

And yet she made enemies at court. The establishment and the court gossips associated flight with decadence and promiscuity. Amyitis's court might be compared with that of the Restoration period, in which most smart people were enjoying sexual excesses under trees in St James's Park while other smart people took the libertines to task for it.

The vertiginous ecstasy of flight, like sexual exuberance, breeds lassitude. Then accidents, syphilis, a weariness-unto-death.

The new inscriptions are in a burial ground close to the city. Perhaps it lay at the foot of the now long-eroded hill.

Example: 'He soared best but fell from grace to dust.' Scholars who wish to discredit Blatter's brilliant thesis argue that these sentiments describe Alexander the Great, who died in Babylon in June 323 BC. But, of course, the inscription refers to a flyer.

They found other bones in the burial ground, tangled – in some cases – with the bones of the crumpled flyers: owls, ostriches, eagles, vultures. And the bones of another creature unknown to modern ornithology. .

Daddy told us bedtime stories like this, asking us to guess which parts were true and which made up. Then he would tell us that actually the Hanging Gardens had been altogether misunderstood – they were nothing more than a warehouse with creeper growing up its sides.

The Babylon Flying Club story was my favourite. I made him tell it again and again, adding details, and refused to voice my instincts about what was invention and what fact. I didn't want them disentangled.

When we were twelve, just before you (you can be Billy too, if you like, but think before you lift the chalice) got to know us, Lizzie was teased at school for those mature breasts of hers which you like so much. Our dormitory companions hoved in on the soft part of her and prodded every night. Lizzie (perhaps as a reprisal for the time when I had told her that if you aren't made up you don't exist) attempted to deflect their attention upon me.

'Laura thinks that people could fly in Ancient Babylon. That they built hills to jump off. Isn't that stupid?'

Joy Fairweather turned to me, intrigued by these new grounds for mockery: 'How, silly?'

I told the story, inventing a pet eagle which Amyitis had brought with her as part of her dowry.

Lizzie had put me up on the high wire above the snake-pit of my listening peers – Joy, Rachel, Alanna, Jessamy and the vicious Daisy who smelt of urine and was probably vicious for that reason.

Telling the story was like flying or sailing, looking to catch the wind and ride a sudden surge or uplift.

'The princess stood at the casement (we had been doing the Eve of St Agnes in English Lit.), surrounded by fruits, unable to conceive a child for Nebuchadnezzar because—'

'She wouldn't have sex,' Joy interrupted. A gale of giggles.

'The princess could not make love because she could not fly and she could not fly because there were no hills and no Median craftsmen to build kites. She wept at the casement, staring out at the plain, at the lights of a caravanserai winding through the night towards the city. She tried to look beyond, towards her distant homeland.'

I told them about John, the president of the flying club, who was the great-great-great-grandfather of Icarus. President John, the princess's lover. I invented a double-harnessed kite under which they flew together.

I looked up to see Lizzie at the back of the group surrounding my bed. In her expression was a confusion of gratitude – I had spared her from being tormented; outrage – I was bastardising one of Daddy's best stories; guilt – she had thrown me to the lions; and envy – I had wrested the storyteller's mantle from Daddy and for once possessed more of him than she did. I became the school minstrel and she remained the girl with big breasts. I am sure it was those breasts which made her starve herself, but the doctors – as you know, Billy – did not agree.

After lights-out, I told them the story of Amyitis's last flight.

'The princess and President John were very good flyers indeed. Even on blustery days, when the rest of the flying club was voluntarily grounded, the lovers would swing high above the desert, defying gravity and Nebuchadnezzar to tear them down.

'A big wind blew from the north-east, on which the princess believed she could smell the pines which forested the hills of Media. She was dizzy with longing – for her childhood. John did not want to go up in the big wind. The princess uncaged her eagle and they watched the regal bird float languidly on the roaring air. She goaded John with the example of the bird.

'The wind seemed to diminish. John and Amyitis were tied into their harnesses, close enough to touch while airborne. A gust snatched them off the hillside, whipping them up and up and up. The air was suddenly thin and cold. The princess drew John closer, to feel his warmth. His hands worshipped her—'

'How do you mean, worshipped?'

'—and they swooned away, from passion and lack of oxygen. Search parties were sent out over the plains. Days passed. Nebuchadnezzar wept on his golden throne. The members of the flying club quit the city, fearing retribution. The lovers were found twenty miles from the city, entwined, tented by the wreckage of their kite. When they took off Amyitis's robe to embalm her they discovered the deformed sprouts of wings growing from her shoulder-blades.'

That distracted the tormentors. But not for long.

Billy really was asleep now, which only proves what a good bedtime story the Babylonian Flying Club is. I don't blame him. I am not after all the easiest person to get along with.

When I find anything in me worth having I gobble it up straight away, not lingering to savour the taste, holding nothing back. What would anyone want with a person like that?

Why must I speak, think, edge out from under the stone which crushes and conceals me, from under silence, to pirouette, speak, think, push against the quiet, against the zinging, whisperless quiet in my head? Why?

I let Billy sleep, moving quietly around our little hotel room, fetching a glass of water and the photographs of my father which I take with me wherever I go.

His face in those photographs – rowing in an eight, doubled over his oar, or kneeling in the garden unpotting a plant – contained a secret potential which his later years failed to unravel. He must have been in his early twenties at the time the photographs were taken. Where did it go, that un-unravelled secret? If Mummy stole it, she never made anything of it – buried it somewhere and then, like a senile dog with an indifferent bone, forgot where. Margaret – his second wife and the nearest thing I have had to a mother – revived a trace of it in him, but never completely. He had a lightness with her sometimes, but it was a levity being weighed on by too many other things. It wasn't just promise or a young man's belief in his future. It was a knowledge he had, which his face declared but hid all at once. As he raised his eyebrows and his eyesockets widened so that his eyes seemed to glow – I can't describe it properly. And then something around his hairline would push the skin back down again. His eyes would retreat and dim, the unravelled thing retrenched, the ramparts reinforced.

Billy had that, almost-beams of light twisting from his eyes. So much brown in them. The marbled brown of his eyes made me think of a school of fish under brackish water – lazy fish, waving in the current, wavering with the river weeds, drifting in formation. I saw the unravelled thing in him and wanted him because of it. And so did Lizzie.

It is there in children – little schools of fish in their eyes, bright and sharp, a moving marble trace in Jimmy's eyes, and Joel's. I could have unwound it in the boys, made then unfreighted men. That's all I was trying to do. I wanted to save them. Tartan Diana will wrap them in barbed wire and feed on them.

I fell asleep beside Billy on the bed. I slipped into a dream in which I saw Tartan Diana – a mixture of Diana and Mummy – arranging flowers in a dark dining room. The smell of wax. A dark wood table. The gold rings on Diana's fingers caught the light. This was a place where the flowers were brought to die. Mummy/Diana was dressing them for death. The garden from which they had been garnered was visible through the windows. The room dark, the scent of the flowers buried by the wax smell, the odour of polish.

Daddy's lawnmower hummed and buzzed in the garden (this blended with the air-conditioning unit sounds in the hotel bedroom).

Daddy's mower imitates the bees, Lizzie said. Aren't children horribly twee? Thinking of sweet things to say, just for the effect their saccharine observations will have on the nearest adult. The procuring of love by any means necessary. Whatever it takes to get a hug, an approving look, any touch of big hands.

There are stones in the garden, marking the line between paddock and lawn. Daddy must have caught one of them with the mower, the blades tearing and shrieking, blunted on the stone. The stone was inside Daddy now, blue lichen crusting its crags and plains. Cold stone chilled his blood. He shivered, a shudder ran through his torso as he lay on the grass.

The stone rolled across me, pinned me to the ground beside him, the blades turning close to us. Men brought more stones, built upon the scarred stone which pressed down on my chest, built around me. I was being built into the city's foundations. Soon the garden was gone, just plots of stone, half-built ramparts.

Men muttered as they worked. Cursed their crude tools, cursed their master. Cursed the king and his daughter.

I saw that my name was carved on each stone. My patronymic name. Blade. Blade. Blade. Blade.

An engineer crouched on the ramparts, calculating the shifts of pressure and mass which took place as I struggled to my feet. Somehow I had found the strength to shoulder the stones, pushing them inside me as if I were an expandable sack. I staggered to the house and looked through the window into the dark dining room where Mummy/Diana had all the flowers lying in heaps on the carpet, on tables, every chair piled high with bouquets of flowers. Her hands were busy, sorting the flowers, making arrangements, setting things straight.

3

I should be flattered by the interest they have shown in my New York adventures. Dario – an Italian boy with pink swollen hands which I think of as his party balloons – quizzed me this morning in pidgin English. I refused to comment. A story cannot be told in the form of an interrogation, and Socratic dialogue is neither my kind of thing nor a form in which Dario is equipped to participate.

Tonight, although conclusions are always an imposition, a way of nipping something in the bud, I must lug the episode towards an ending. The three braided Frenchmen take the boat back to Mykonos tomorrow and I have promised them closure (as the French put it when forced to speak English) before they depart. I hope I have the bottle to tell them the rest of it.

The wind has failed to drop this evening. It tears at the palm leaves above the terrace, whisks butt-ends from ashtrays and snatches towels from balcony railings. The waves in the bay are laid out like lines of a prohibited substance on an azure mirror. Geranium petals blotch the terrace like poppies in a foreign field.

Every Greek island has its Homer's tomb and this one is no exception. Either – as a number of scholars have cogently argued – there were as many Homers as there are islands or this is yet another example of the historical possessiveness by which we hope, in claiming to own some part of the past, to reclaim it for ourselves alone, excluding others from its shaded gardens.

I have been sent on a visit to this island's Homer's tomb by the hotelier Franz Marelli-Kreitznacht. He is keen to interest me in burial; and, I can only suppose, in the deaths by which burial is necessarily preceded. Homer's tomb is no more than a bunch of rocks and a shallow cave pebbled by goat's droppings.

The guests are a mawkish lot and I had wanted to cheer them up by telling them about New York, but I'm not doing terribly well. My story was supposed to be happy, but the truth is sad. When they were all settled in the circle, I started to tell them the hard bit:

When I awoke from the dream of Mummy/Diana and the flower-morgue, Billy was no longer beside me on the bed. I sat upright and waited for the feeling of being in a hotel room in New York to predominate over the dream sensation of walking around stuffed full of stones.

When I was able to move, I went to the bathroom. I noticed a note on the floor by the bathroom door: 'Base 6 – W41st and Broadway. See u there?'

It turned out to be a nightclub. Once I had passed the style-and-cash test at the door and adjusted to the flashing lights, I was able to see Billy on the dance floor wearing my Babylon Flying Club T-shirt. Or rather, he was in the middle of taking it off and swapping it with a girl whose name turned out to be Rae-Ann.

He had probably worn the T-shirt in the hope of soliciting just this sort of exchange. There they were at the edge of the dance floor – two footballers after the final whistle, exchanging shirts as mementoes. Rae-Ann had my shirt half over her head and so did not see me arrive. Billy watched me sizing up her unfettered breasts – as full and heavy as Lizzie's had once been. I snatched the shirt from her and stomped off.

Although I had stolen what was mine, the true theft being Billy's attempted gift to Rae-Ann, I had the same sensation as when I am floating through the doors of a Knightsbridge store with a silk blouse stuffed under my skirt, wondering if I will set off the security alarm.

When I looked back, Rae-Ann was clawing at Billy's chest to get her shirt back, her tits flapping in agitation. Billy was laughing. Billy Lizzie Tartan Diana – traitors all. I should have left New York then. Packed and caught the next flight. But I lingered outside the club, waiting for Billy and Rae-Ann, hoping that he would emerge without her, in search of me.

Outside the club, squatting in the street with my back against a cold wall, within the protectorate of the bouncers' attack-zone, I imagined them dancing inside, him bare-chested now.

I am blessed with the ability to squat comfortably on my haunches for hours at a time: flat feet and double-jointed hips; or, more romantically, a nomadic nature.

Yellow cabs bounced along the street, slouchy, slowing at the club's entrance, whoring for a ride. The bouncers waved them on. Three boys came to the door with false ID. Money rustled and the bouncers let them in. As the door opened the previously muffled music swelled into the street. I ducked involuntarily.

Did it matter that Billy was fondling Rae-Ann or that she thought me a bitch for walking off with the shirt, my shirt, or that Amyitis died in airborne flagrante with her father John?

None of it mattered much as I squatted alone outside a nightclub on Broadway.

What mattered was the sensation of shifting, like sand being pulled away from around my feet by the drag of a retreating wave. Or the feeling when the train next to yours moves off and you are sure for a moment that it is your train which is in motion; then, the little twinge as your mind assigns the mobility to the other train and you lose your balance in the realisation that you have not moved at all.

It has been away from this shifting, dragging, twingeing that I have always sought to fly. Up in the air the ground can hardly shift beneath your feet. The air is always slipping and sliding but that is exactly what it is supposed to do – shift, shimmy, roar; tumble, roil.

I followed Billy and Rae-Ann. Not so much to spy – I had already seen more than I wanted to and guessed the rest – but to slip out of always being the onlooker. To get involved. You know how they tell depressives to get involved? Involved in the community. Not that I'm – oh, fuck it.

Rae-Ann and Billy could hardly go to the hotel where Billy must have assumed that I would be waiting for him. She had reappropriated her T-shirt while he wore a new red shirt which carried the logo of the club – Base 6 – from which they had just so jointly and charmingly egressed.

Rae-Ann was the type Billy and Daddy and Vivian and all the rest of the boys seem to go for in the short term. And don't they just love the short term? A girl with a short half-life. They like that sort of girl and that sort of girl likes them – but not for long because in the end who do Billy and Vivian and Daddy really want? A long-term girl, a girl with flair, a girl with claws under the varnish, bite under the lipgloss. A somebody like me.

Rae-Ann was all cunt and of that they tire, although I wonder if they secretly wish that I was just cunt and being more than that is a handicap. Laura can be so tiresome, so contrary – such a difficult girl.

She was acting drunker than she was, but was quite drunk enough for what Billy, who was high from the painkillers, had in mind for her. I was sober as a pilot.

If they are lucky, the Rae-Anns turn into Tartan Dianas. And if they cannot find the dick to buy the rock, they go on being Rae-Anns. When they are older, when pussy alone will not serve, they get lonely.

We were in procession up Broadway, Rae-Ann's hand on Billy's buttock, squeezing, Billy probably thinking beyond fucking her to how to get rid of her afterwards. She was in a haze of numinous excitement, beyond which she could not see. Billy would have told her by now about all the things he wanted to do to her and how big his cock was and how hard it was getting just thinking about doing those things to her. She would have giggled when he told her what he planned to do and now she would be wondering whether she would actually – I mean, really-really – let him. But she wouldn't think it through too far, knowing that she would let him do it in the end and that to decide not to and then let him would make her feel sad and confused the next day (and Texan girls don't like to feel sad or confused), whereas just to do it, or let him do it, would be wicked. Something to whisper to her girlfriends back in Houston. And the girlfriends would say, No, you didn't, you let him? That? Rae-Ann would smile and say, You should try it, honey.

It was this reaction which Billy relied upon in a Rae-Ann. Being trained to take advantage of people, he made them feel that the thing he threatened to do to them was the very forbidden thing for which they had always longed. Thus he could pose as St George and still play the dragon.

In the fifties they turned west and walked into the foyer of a midtown chain hotel. I went straight to the lifts while Rae-Ann fetched her key from reception. An African couple came to the lift and stood beside me. Then two gays in white jeans. Rae-Ann and Billy were kissing in the middle of the foyer. Then they headed for the lift, not seeing me behind the Africans.

The lift doors opened. Billy and Rae-Ann slipped in. A hotel man touched my arm—

'Are you a resident here, miss?'

I lunged for the lift as the doors began to close but one of the queens was in my way. My sudden movement unbalanced the African woman in her long jungle-kit. Rae-Ann shrieked.

'Bitch,' I yelled as the doors slid shut.

'Please, miss,' the hotel man said. 'This is a hotel.'

When I regained my hotel room, all the lights were off except in the bathroom. I found his Percoset and took three, pocketing the rest. A hip flask of vodka by the fridge. I slugged. In the bathroom I gathered my hair into a mane. Thickly matted in places, it dropped to the middle of my back when I released it.

Some people need children to keep them on the rails, to keep them focused on the future – Joel and Jimmy, Katherine, Isabel, Billy, even Rae-Ann. Someone to look out for, to worry about, to ask me will it be all right, will everything work out?

I remember very clearly what was passing through my mind that night in New York. I was thinking about Daddy and Lizzie. Partly because being with Billy was a bit like being Lizzie myself. He only really wanted to spend time with me because it was easy to pretend that I was her.

I must take you back, now, to my twelfth year, in which my twin sister Lizzie and I lived during the weekends with our father and his new wife Margaret. The Margaret who had once been our nanny. She still had a separate bedroom in the house as well as the one she shared with Daddy. Sometimes he would go to her in her old nanny bedroom. One listless summer afternoon I squatted outside Margaret's room waiting for something to happen. Do you remember how much of being twelve consisted of waiting to be grown up?

Margaret's door was locked and Daddy would not come

out. I heard the grunts and squeals of trapped animals behind the door, confusing to my childish ears.

That feeling when the train next to yours moves off and you are sure for a moment that it is your train which is in motion; then, the little twinge as your mind assigns the mobility to the other train and you lose your balance in the realisation that you have not moved at all.

I was clutching my doll, whose name was Missy.

There is a murmuring from across the circle on the terrace, a sob from Brigitte which harmonises with the groaning of the wind.

Please do not interrupt, I say to her. At moments like this I cannot manage if you interrupt.

Preceded by a muffled clatter, Daddy burst out of Margaret's room and strode straight past me. He was followed by Lizzie who stopped and glanced down at me with a look of possessive triumph, holding a sheet around her narrow shoulders.

Here was my frail, big-breasted Lizzie, not the Margaret I had been imagining.

I followed him. Not so much to spy – I had already seen more than I wanted to and guessed the rest – but to slip out of always being the onlooker. To get involved.

Daddy was in his dressing room changing his shirt. He asked me about the afternoon – I had been swimming at a friend's house and had walked home early over the fields. I could not answer his questions. I wanted him, more than anything else, to tell the Median princess story. To tell it to me only.

'I want you—'

'Come with me to collect Margaret?' Daddy was fiddling with a cufflink, having trouble inserting it into the tight slot in the cuff.

'I want you to tell me the princess story.'

'You're too old for that story now.'

'Is Lizzie too old for it?' I asked. 'Or too young?'

'It has always been your story, Lorry,' Daddy said. 'You made it your own—'

'And Lizzie has made you hers.'

'Lorry—'

'—for the afternoon. Of course you would. You are so much more alike. So much better matched. I can just see how terribly compatible and everything you are—'

'Stop.'

'You adore adoring each other so much more than you adore me or Margaret for that matter and I suppose talking of Margaret that I should explain to her how much more than her and me you adore Lizzie. So that she knows where she stands. Or falls. Perhaps you should explain the falling part to her.'

'Sit—'

'What am I, your dog?'

'—down.' There was nowhere but the single bed that Daddy had used during the last year of his marriage to Mummy.

He sat down beside me, the collar of his shirt up, pushing his hair up at the back. The hair on his forearms was thick and curled. He smelt of my sister. Our arms and knees touched. I pretended we were in a cinema together, the mirror before us a screen on which I could see a handsome man in his forties and a strange young girl sitting beside one another on a narrow bed. It seemed to me that the next thing the couple would do – for a couple I assumed them to be – was to kiss.

I waited until the young girl on the cinema screen turned to the middle-aged man beside her on the narrow bed, looking up at her father, her neck twisting, for guidance – it seemed she wanted guidance, wanted him to sanction some thought of hers, allow her some treat or favour.

'Please, Daddy.' I glanced at the mirror as I spoke,

hoping to find in the reflection of my father's features something more than I saw in the original. But even his reflection was weighed with stony heaviness, a look of grinding submission, the spirit wrestled to the ground. I shuddered against his coldness, sensing the chill in his shadow. I shuddered and wept.

At last, he spoke to me:

The princess begged her father to join her in Babylon. He came in disguise, not wishing to be hampered by the courtesies his royal blood required, posing as the flying instructor who would train the Babylonian Flying Club.

Only high in the air, hanging below the double-harnessed kite, could the princess and her father acknowledge one another. Under this constraint his secret presence brought them grief and joy in equal measure; much of the time they were in one another's company but forced to deny the truth of his identity. This seemed to her a form of treachery. She wanted to bring him into the open, unmask him, have his presence known and celebrated, and yet to do so would deprive her of having that part of him which she had absolutely and which he reserved for her alone.

Below the kite, they would twist around in the harnesses to touch one another, to embrace. Their movements were restricted by the arrangement of the straps and the delicacy of balance required to sustain windborne flight. Their longing ballooned in the air where it was given its strictured opportunity, each touch, each kiss something less than enough. He gave her a green emerald which she kept against her skin. At night, missing him, she would press the emerald to her flesh.

My body relaxed against my father's. My head rested upon his lap now. I felt sleepy and safe.

*   *   *

They recognised the wind beating on them as a force equivalent to that which they withheld from one another. They became blind to danger, risking their last flight together when the rest of the club was voluntarily grounded. They twisted in the harnesses, loosening the straps to be closer.

A maddened burst of air, pulling sharp showers of sand from the desert floor, tumbled the kite. The flyers swung wildly in their harnesses, the king gripping his girl by the mane of her hair. The hem of her robe snapped from his grasp. Her thighs shone in the high light. Still he clung to her mane and she dangled, his eyes always upon her as time stretched until he smelt the pines, the taste of pistachio in his mouth, saw the day of her birth, of his investiture, the face of the brother he had killed to claim the throne.

For a miraculous moment the kite settled back on the wind. Then a gust flipped it backwards into a juddering dive.

She believed that they would strike water. (She saw below them – or was it above? – the lake in which she had swum as a child, her mother's shawl on the bank, her ayah bending over the cot, peacocks waking her in the night and their feathers made into a robe for her sixth birthday.) The splash and then the cool of it, her father cutting away the harness and swimming with her to the surface. Her last thought was of the emerald which she dropped as she saw not water but sand accelerating towards them. She watched the emerald drop through blue water to settle in the spines of a sea-urchin. It would be safe there. And then nothing.

A new voice surprised us: 'I don't see why they have to die.'

Lizzie. Listening in.

Daddy stood up. It was as if he had forgotten that my head was resting on his lap. I let my head rise with his rising body and fall, inert on the bed.

Daddy approached the mirror, running his hands through

his hair, rubbing his hand across his mouth, inspecting the invisible stain slicked on his palm. Behind him, I was gazing at the floor, my foot kicking spasmodically at the carpet.

'Fetch me a drink, would you, Lorry?' Daddy straightened his collar, buttoned it and ran his fingers along a rack of ties.

'Please don't call me Lorry.'

'I mean it affectionately.'

'Why,' I asked him, 'if you do it with her – what's wrong with me?'

That was what I thought about in the bathroom in New York in the middle of the night. The question I had asked my father I had asked of Billy too.

Enough, frankly, was enough.

I was planning a fresh start. That hour (three in the morning), that bathroom (cream and chrome), those scissors (Sheffield steel and matt-black handles), that razor (Billy's and of uncertain provenance). Without an audience, without commentary and – please – without lament.

Brigitte restrained her snivelling.

The smell of Billy's urine. I flushed it for him. He should wear nappies. I could change them for him.

Then I cut everything to just below the ear.

Not sufficient. What remained looked thatched, superfluous.

People say things like, I need my own space. I need to spend time with myself, just being with myself, just sitting with my feelings. Lonely little people not managing to sit with themselves, always standing up and walking away from themselves but sure they should have sat with themselves, sure that if they had listened to the quiet voices then benediction – whispered, soothing, final – might somehow be heard.

But there is only static, like the white noise in cathedrals, the slightly singing hum of echoed steps and whispers which approximates silence and respect. That churchy sound promises something but I never heard God speak there. Did you?

Talking of which, there is a black Afrocentric historian who writes that the Egyptians who were – didn't you know? – black Africans, not olive-skinned types, invented gliders and used them successfully. There is also a man who has recently developed a device called an Ornithopter which gives humans the capacity to fly as birds fly. It won't be long; our ascendancy is promised.

I am trying to stay in my own voice, to sit with myself (in my own space, not running away, you should note, waiting for whispers of approbation, approval or even that elusive benediction). My words shiver and twitch, rustling in the draught from the air-conditioning.

Lizzie's voice is close enough to mine in tone and timbre that I can pretend to be her on the telephone (and she me, of course) if the need or whim should arise. We played havoc with Daddy in this way. But Lizzie, a student of excess, has abused the confusion of voices.

I did not need a voice to cut my hair.

Perhaps cutting it would help to quieten the other voices, I thought, shock them into silence. So many people muttering all at once and with so much to say.

I reduced my hair to an uneven stubble, whipped up a lather on Billy's shaving brush and worked a helmet of foam on to my head. The rasp of the razor through the foam was delicious, like mowing a lawn of dry spring grass.

Look what Billy has done. Billy and Daddy between them. Look at this ruined head, look at my bald ridiculous head and the cuts where his razor has slashed into my scalp and hurt me. Look at what he has achieved.

They must have been looking for me after the Met. But they had no name. Thankfully. The boys had not asked my name. I was as nameless as the man cutting his hair outside the museum. He and I were equally nameless.

Should I have shaved my eyebrows? What do *you* think?

Looking in the mirror, I thought about the way we had spied on the man at the museum whose mirror had been our window. Are there others watching me, gloating, feeding on me? I tried to push a toothbrush between the wall and the mirror but the casing was flush against the surrounding tiles, leaving no edge for purchase. I began to see faint silhouettes – Joy Fairweather from school, the chauffeur, Tartan Diana – in the deep background of the mirror.

On or off?

The eyebrows. Try to concentrate.

All right, Daddy. If you say so.

And off they came, with two deft swoops of the razor.

I was scary. I scared myself. I avoided mirrors.

And then I went and got fat. Fat as fat can be.

And then, a few months later, I met Vivian.

4

Vivian Black

The name is Vivian. Like the cricketer. Now there's a gentleman. And I won't have no trouble. Not in my motor. That's where I set the rules. If I fancy a chat, all well and good. Otherwise, shut it.

It's a matter of respect, really. I got my dignity.

Don't matter where I come from, you got mixed blood in this country means you come from nowhere and anywhere. Who gives a fuck? Too black for the whites, too white for the brothers.

Not brothers to me they ain't.

'I've got three waiting on the shop, a Fulham Broadway in ten minutes, two cars for Portobello and a Richmond – somebody call me.'

Never look back, that's my motto. Be conscious? Get political? Life can be sweet, why fuck about with it?

*　　*　　*

'Ninety-six, you picked up yet?'

'Ninety-six still waiting to pick up,' I said into the handset.

She was a fat cunt first time she got in my cab. Had to push the front seat right forward to fit her thighs in the back.

You must be joking. Wouldn't of fucked Laura to save the planet. Not for five hundred quid. Snotty cow. Driver, she went. Tek me to Knaytsbridge. Wait here, driver. Get me that Vivian, she said. He makes me laugh. Her clown. Her fool. Training to be a pilot. So she said. Thought she knew a thing or two about theft. I give her one or two tips. Good nerve, I give you that. Steady. Cold in the blood. Face. She can face a person off. I admire that, even in a bird.

He's an animal, that Vivian. That's what she thought.

No, I could see her thinking it.

But in the end, what's so ghastly – that's a word she'd use – about that? He's not as stupid as he looks. Who knows, Mummy might take to him.

The airport. Only punter I ever had wanted the airport wait and return was Laura. Not picking anyone up, just go to Heathrow, then come back. Done that a few times.

She was a fat cunt 'n' all. Perfectly true. Wedged herself in the back. But she had it, even with carrying all that flab. Must of been fourteen stone of it wobbling about. The motor handled different. Honest. But the look. She had the look.

And the mouth. Little creases in the corners, twitching them. Catching my eye in the mirror. Kind of hello-are-you-up-for-it look which any wolf will recognise, being as it takes one to know one. Very like a bloke she was in that respect.

Sometimes, when I'm beefing a bird, it feels like I've got a spoon stuck to me instead of a dick and I'm scooping something out of her. When I've finished I've got a bit of her she never meant to give away – vanilla ice-cream.

And after, I haven't got it neither – cos it's melted. And sometimes it's chocolate ice-cream. Depending.

You think I'm crude, go down the office meet some of the other drivers. A bunch of nobodies just like you. You'd get along fine.

You're all cunts, and half of you don't know it. Punters. It's the belief. That's what does me in. The shit you believe in. Family values. Law and order. The role of the police. The fine-tuning of the economy. Democracy. Ha-fucking-ha. Know who started that lark? Five centuries before baby Jesus? The Athenians. Worked all right for them cos they had slaves and women couldn't vote. Must of made things a fuck sight easier. They was shirt-lifters 'n' all. But they wouldn't have you fucking the slaves. Oh no, mate, that was bang out of order. Don't learn about that watching *Eastenders*. Some of it I got from that Bernal book what I read inside. The rest was Laura. She was into it – Greeks and Romans and that.

She'd watch me in the mirror with that don't-think-I-don't-know-exactly-what-the-fuck-you're-thinking look. Not that I was thinking it. But I liked it. First time with her was to Heathrow, as I said. To watch the aeroplanes. Like a six-year-old. Made me park up and stand there with her, watching the runway. Got me on to hostesses. Which ones I fancied. Did I ever? What was it like? And when she was about to – you know – what did you think? Laura asked. Think? I was making it up as I went along – din want to let her down, in I? – never having had the pleasure with a stewardess in mid-air (the ground being another matter), so I could say whatever come into my head.

This is a bit odd, all right?

I wanted to say to her, Kill me, go on, try to fucking top me, strangle me, fucking hurt me.

Go on, Laura said.

That's it, I said.

I'm not as fat as you think I am, she said.

You are very fucking fat indeed, I said. Then I drove her back to town.

Some birds, you can have what they call a full and frank exchange. I mean, talk about not just sex but everything under the sun, under the belt. She come out with things, out of the blue. That first time, driving back to town, she was on about Dionysus, this Greek piss-artist used to rip the living heart out of a creature, chew on it. Just like that, by Heston services. What can you say? The answer is, a person who talks like that you can say anything you want. Which is how we become friends.

They get off on it, see? He's just the driver, he don't mean nothing, just part of the furniture. It's not personal, that's just how they see me. Tell me stuff they wouldn't never tell anyone else, act out of character. And I get the benefit.

A man I once knew – he was a chaplain, as it happens – told me a sin is just a mistake before God. Mistakes, I worked out myself, come from stupidity. So evil is stupidity and the other way round. Got it?

Are you listening, Laura? I got better things to do than talk to the rear-view mirror.

Well, look like you are. What you after, then? Sex, is it? You want to hear about women? Black women and white men; women and dogs; women and gorillas; women and women? I'll give you women.

People are basic.

Yeah, and proud of it. Basic, but not stupid.

What? You fucking what?

Not any more. Not since I done that last stretch.

You and your mouth, Viv. Unbelievable.

* * *

I done more porridge than the three bears. The last suspended finished seven years ago. Know what I mean?

Have to explain it all from scratch, in I?

Seven years after the last sentence is finished you got a clean slate. No jacket, as the Americans like to say.

No, I'm no villain. Never was a fucking villain. Never done nothing I wouldn't do again. No regrets.

Leave it there, son. She don't want to know.

Well, there was one or two things. The bloke with his hands nailed to the side of the goods van, me holding the hammer and him screaming 'I never bought a car from your fucking brother. You got the wrong bloke.' What the fuck, they all say that. I shine the torch in his face, have a butcher's.

It is the wrong fucking bloke an all. Trouble was, once the nails is in, it ain't so easy getting them out again. So we scarpered. Left him to it.

That's more like an occupational hazard. Not villainy. Could we leave it there? I said. Drop it, all right?

Plenty of violence to come. Be patient, willya? I should nut you. Have a bit of bleeding respect or I will nut you. Don't believe me? Come here then, you cunt.

All right, all right, all right. Just don't wind me up. Let's stick to the present. Where we're at.

I got plenty of better things to do. Yes, I have.

Where did a person like you learn to speak like that? I'd like a word with your mother. She should be ashamed. Of you and her both. Mine?

Mine?

Grandad was a Jamaican scouser. Come over to Liverpool docks in the hold of a banana boat. He never sussed it was refrigerated till after they set sail, hatches battened down. Shorts and a thin shirt. Him and his mates banging away on the underside of the deck for a day. Got him ready for the climate, that's what he said, but fuck me, can you imagine it? Arrived in Liverpool, it was snowing. He'd never seen snow where he come from. Fuck me, he said to himself.

He knocked up this fancy bird from the Wirral – liked a bit of dark flesh, you understand, used to smoke a likka bitta weed with me granddad. He give her one, put a baby on her.

The accent changes cos that's part of me. Got a bitta yard, in I. Yard, scouse, cockney. I been in the melting-pot.

Me mum, God bless her, is a brown woman and Da was this cunt of a docker used to lie and cheat and generally diss her.

To disrespect. Diss. See? Where you been all your life, in a convent? In Surrey?

He was a proper bastard. Wanted me to look a lot whiter than what I look. Wouldn't take me to the football cos he was ashamed. Didn't want people calling him a monkey-fucker. Which is why I don't support Liverpool. Never took me to Anfield. Not once. Fuck him, I thought, and went off to Old Trafford with Desmond.

My cousin Des. Blacker than your little ankle boots, Des. Same grandma and grandad but he come out like a country-born Jamaican. Me, I'm a brown man. Desmond is black. And righteous with it.

He calls me Iscariot. Hey, yo, Judas man. What's happenin', white boy? You mofuck white man, diss your breddah in yard. Fuck off, Desmond. Fuck right off.

Called me a racist bastard. Literally accurate enough. Had to knock him about a bit. It's all right having family work for you. But not stupid black family. Doing a bit of bird now, is Des, which proves my point. No, I don't want to talk about it.

Shut the fuck up a minute, will you?

It was a small man's crime. Stuff I used to do before I knew any better. No rumbling sub-post offices in Stockport (I never got done for that, so you stay schtum).

And if you think you can grass me up cos you're a bird, let me tell you this: some people won't hit women never. Whatever they done. Some men hit women all the time – like Scottish John from the TC. If a woman wants to be hit? Hit it.

They love it.

No?

That's bollocks. I got this girl I know in Watford. See her say once a month, when the work drives me that way. I go in the house, give her a good hiding. After that she come soon as I touch her. She fucking loves it.

You want some?

I bet you fucking do.

Never let yourself think about it? Well, think about it.

If a woman fucks your mate while she's being fucked by you: hit her and hit your mate. If a woman grasses you up, hit her. Otherwise: don't hit her. It's simple.

I'd never hit me mum, whatever she done. Know what she used to call me? On account of my family name was Black. Vivian, like the cricketer – Black. She only goes and marries a white docker called Black. Could of fucking thought ahead a few inches. Blackie, they called me in the yard at school – even the black kids. Fucking nerve.

No one calls me that no more. Except one bird, the only bird apart from me mum I won't hit. No, I don't want—

Will you just leave it with the questions? You people should be locked up. Teach you a thing or two.

The thing with the trains, that was well stupid. My brother Kenny, he's in the motor trade up near Chester. Three forecourts, local clout, delivery mileage Jags to local businessmen and ex-fleet Sierras on the never to anyone who has a few quid for the deposit.

Kenny's got a lovely mouth on him. Sell salt water to the navy. But soft when it comes to collection. People, they buy a motor on the never, get behind on the payments – yeah, life's shit – go quiet and disappear. Kenny bells me:

got another defaulter, give me a name and address to start
from. Wants his instalments, don't want to know how I
come by 'em. Don't tell me nothing, Viv, he goes. What
the eye can't see.

Free-range law enforcement, that's me. Was me. Me and
my posse. They was rough lads, let's face it. Liked to think
up new ways of collecting a debt. Use their imagination.
Hard men, they were, and I was the leader of these hard
men. Hard but stupid.

Kenny and me, two sides of the same coin: I done fifteen
of the last twenty-five years inside; Kenny just got on the
local council last year, sitting on the board of guvnors at his
kids' school.

So we nailed this bloke to a train by his hands. Three-
inch nails.

But he was the wrong bloke.

Why should I? Think of all the ones what got away. Only
bad I feel is it was stupid. His brother was local CID which
didn't help.

Chain 'em to the back of the Land Rover, drive around a
field. Or shoot 'em up with a bit of gear, make them pay for
that an' all. Put them in the meat room down the market
overnight. Dangle 'em from bridges. Then there was the
rabid dog. Tie the bloke to a chair. Bring in the dog on
a chain. Barking, jumping about, lunging at the punter.
Then my mate Jimmy would say he's got one of us already
and bring me in shuddering and shaking and frothing at the
mouth, eyeballs flying about. They paid up. Every last one
of 'em.

Twenty per cent. Of each payment we got back. It was
just business. And we got done for it. GBH. Kidnap.

You could say we done it for the money, but that's not
it. It's a bit like fucking a bird up the arse. Not so much the
pleasure but the power.

You ever taken it?

Who don't want to answer questions now, eh? Don't be

shy. Dark, like me, rich and dark. If the Greeks done it it's all right with me. They was all from the black, 'n' all. This bloke wrote a book about it. The brothers was circulating it inside. Bernal, that was the name.

Now, the sub-post office. That was a crime to remember. I was driving. Supposed to be. This bloke Gav, when we get there he drops his bottle so I have to stave in the windows and stand guard. Even stupid villains can get along if they don't drop their bottle. But Gav, he was finished from that night. Runs a pub now, in Hartlepool.

We done all right. Tooling along the M62, counting the swag. Then this speed chaser – tuned-up Beemer like the one what I've got now – come after us. Never gonna beat him in a straight run. Not in a Daimler. I come off the next exit, spin the canoe on the ramp in the wet, run it along the barrier facing backwards. Shrieking noise worser than a bastard. Flip it round again.

I nipped into a housing estate. Plenty of side streets – lose the rozzers. Park up. Lads jump out the canoe.

Jew canoe. Daimler. V12. Some of my best mates. No offence.

Lads arguing over the swag, panicking, running. I grab a wad of twenties and scarper, each man for himself. Make a couple of turns and roll under a motor. Just my luck, oil dripping from the sump on to my boat. Wet tarmac and the glow from the neon lamps shining in the wet on the tarmac. Fucking cold. I could of used a stiff drink and a fag.

Well, they grabbed Steve straight off. Way I heard it, Steve told them he was out walking the dog. What dog, sir? I lost it, guv. Can't find the little mutt nowhere.

Shut up, sonny. You're nicked.

Then more sirens as the local bill get called in. Me under this rusty old Triumph Dolomite, I fancy it was – dealing with the fear. Not a move, not a single twitch.

Under a motor, in the wet, black engine oil dripping on my cheek, at liberty, a wedge in my pocket.

Unfuckingbelievable feeling. Watch the rozzers' boots approach, near enough to lick, them trying to decide is there another villain come out the canoe. Just as well there wasn't no dogs, or that'd be me fucked. Teeth chattering, clamp the jaw shut. Nerve held. Four hours later they give it up.

I come out at dawn. Walk to the motorway. Hitch to Manchester, get this script off a doctor I knew. A reward to myself, see? Eight days later I got done for assaulting an officer outside a pub in Blackburn. On remand over Christmas. Then back inside.

But the post office. I felt alive. Stupid, maybe, but very fucking alive. That's what you have to overcome. Bad judgment looking for thrills.

That was then and now is minicabbing. Here's a rule: have a sound reason for every iffy thing you do. You like that?

What sort of things? Well, fucking someone else's woman. Give her a lift home. Help her in with the shopping. Give her one in the utility room, up on the washing machine during the spin cycle, Sainsbury's bags around in a circle. They all want to see how much of it they can take. What am I doing there? Just the driver, mate, don't mind me.

Or let's say I have a friend, not that I necessarily do, mind you. He's a fence. Needs to get here and there, ducking and diving about town. Collect, sell, deliver. I don't know nothing about it, love. Job come through the office.

Dealers, pimps, tarts, lifters.

I wouldn't have no fucking shirtlifters on board. Catch some manky disease.

Shoplifters.

Here's a tenner. Wait for me. Come bucketing out, back door open at the ready. And if they get done, I'm not associated. But the fee's the same. Plus plenty of reading time.

Never touch them. Look what they done. As a form of commercial enterprise? High risk, high return. Very nasty type of personnel involved. Better off investing in me than in drugs. Low risk, high return. Buy me a second motor, then a minicab office. Geezer I know should be out next week, he'd be the perfect controller.

Script? That was strictly medication. Keeping things on an even keel. The difference? Recreation and medication. Don't take this personally, but why don't you just fuck off now? Go and quiz someone else, you've had your ten pence worth.

I'll smoke me own.

When I was a kid.

All the other kids was doing a bit of blow. Blues. Look, fuck off, will you? I don't need this.

Sometimes it's sweet to talk to a pretty girl.

Yes, I do.

Look at her tits when she's saying things. Think about fucking her.

Don't be flattered. I never don't think about it, even if she's a dog. It's automatic, like picking my nose.

I don't think that hurts nobody. You want to be hurt, is that it? When was the last time? All right, then, who with?

Don't like it, do you? Yeah, I think you're scared. Of what you might do if you let yourself.

Get out, then. I told you to fuck off anyway. I said fuck off, din I? Stay or go, I don't give a bollocks. But decide. I got a life.

Yes I am. Cos you assumed I'd be stupid and you give me that sarcastic look like you got a pencil stuck up your arse. Now I hold the pencil. And when I get the urge I give it a shove. Treat me like a cunt, I'll act like a cunt. It grates for a bit and then you like it, hearing all them things said that the people you associate with won't say. Cos they got pencils up their arses an all. Gis a fag.

That's eight quid. Plus the waiting time.

Well, thanks very much, then.

Squirming by the end of it she was. I had her squirming in her seat and if I'd of stuck my mitt in her mop I could of give her one then and there. But I'm not bothered. Let it wait. Let her beg for it. It'll be better if she begs. Thinks I'm an animal. She can think what she likes. She's fat.

Nailing the wrong bloke to the train. Now why did I tell her that? Still proud of it, I spose, cos I done it without fear. Never a moment of fear that night. Think about him more than the ones who never made it, more than the ones what croaked. I never set out to kill, not in cold blood. But things happen. Things just fuck up in front of your face. People fuck up. Choosing the right people is a way of getting beyond stupid villainy. How do you know in advance what a bloke is gonna be like on the night? Fuck me if I know.

Times I've had the fear worse that anything is over a little nothing. Like the time me 'n' Dean done the doctor up in Lancaster. Very simple crime, very stupid. And we fucked it up. Dean's in America, with the Colombians. Unless they topped him by now. Probably tops them just for the hell of it. Dean's a five-star cunt if ever there was.

Why should the doctor give me no peace when some of the others lie still? Doctor's alive, probly lecturing users about clean needles, bogging around, being a professional.

With the satisfaction, the added value, of knowing he put me 'n' Dean behind bars.

Dean looks like a Muppet, thick curly hair cut just below the ears. Flops about when he gets excitable. Big lad, used to be a fairish centre forward. About as educated as a piece of shit, except when it comes to drugs – subscribed to that MIMS what the doctors use – and guns. 'Part from that he don't know nothing about life you can't get from watching Jean-Claude Van Damme movies. It's all there, Viv. You should give him a look. Kill you soon as shake your hand.

The knack is to seem like you will – like you would at the drop of a hat – without ever having to do it. The chill. If they force you to do it, then you've fucked it. Took me time and bodies to learn that. Time and bodies.

In me big motor where you can't touch me. You bunch of addled old cunts. All of you. Yeah, you 'n' all. In me big motor where you can't touch me.

'Morning, ninety-six.' The controller on the two-way. Whoosh and crackle behind his voice.

'Fuck off, Tom.'

'Fuck you 'n' all, Viv,' goes the controller. 'Job on the shop if you want it.' Four in the morning, what sort of job is likely to be worth taking off for the shop this time of day? Piss-artists. And arguments – girlfriend slung out, dodgy bloke looking for skirt. I'll cruise it.

Me motor – Laura, she calls it Kevin. Looks like a piece of shit – authentic inner London: rust on the boot-rim, big knock on the passenger door, couple of key-scratches down the side (done them myself), rear light housing cracked till the next MOT. Changed the 535i badge for 518 so it looks poxy and underpowered, which it ain't. Goes like a bird fucking on speed. And faster. Leather seats in front. Replaceable cloth in the back for the punters. Dark blue exterior – not too flash, not too spade, not too *bad*, as the brothers say.

Call me anything you want but a spade I ain't. Or at least call me a black man. A conscious fucking black man. Not some git in a poncy motor getting pulled every night for holding a bit of blow. None of your 'yo' shit. No Tom on the chest, no embossed baseball cap, no big watch, none of that music pumping out the car as if to say look what a lot of fucking noise I make I must have a dick the size of a telephone pole.

That's Desmond down to a T. Hello, Des, welcome to the show.

Not that I mind them blokes – charging about like a bunch of girls saying arrest me, arrest me, look at me officer I just done a crime or about to do one at any rate, why not fucking arrest me before I even think about it? Keeps the rozzers busy. Why not? It's a free country. Good luck to 'em.

Meaner 'n shit on the inside. I've shared cells. Bang them up, they fester and rot. Pining for the savannah, need to have a bit of a wander. Start to smell different when you bang 'em up. They get the 'ump something horrible. Fuck 'em.

Yeah, it's happened to me. Claustrophobic body-odour condition, that's what the wife calls it. Even she had trouble coming near me during visits. You don't need to know nothing about her. Forget I mentioned her. Just drop it, all right?

'Ninety-six on the shop now.'

I'm staying schtum. Best time of day, this. Good for starting but better for finishing. No traffic, dawn soon. Got the road to yourself. End of a big Saturday night, frinstance, drop the last punter and cruise till the light come up. Go up west get the papers for her indoors. She likes them colour books they do of a Sunday. Get the news off the radio myself.

'Ninety-six.'

Might just give that Tonia a quick one. Bird I know over Holland Park way. Fancy. The husband off on business.

Eindhoven. Paris. Clocked him for a pansy even if she says his tool works. I've had him on board. Earning all that wedge, can't tell when his wife's being stuffed by a half-caste cabbie with a record longer than the A13. Antonia. Where do they get names like that? Punch her up on the mobile, see what gives.

Why does it make that noise? I mean them particular tones, you know, when you plug in the numbers and it plays a little seven-note tune? I'll ask her husband. He'll know.

'Tone? Viv . . . You want me or what? . . . Nah. But it could be . . . Just started.' Got her kid up with the 'flu. 'Why should I fucking save it? . . . Yeah, for anyone . . . Bye, doll.' Fuck her for hours, bitch won't come. Then I stuck a couple of fingers up her arse – her fighting me like a cat – she come straight off. Predictable, really.

Well, excuse me, ladies.

And all that follows from that first little excursion. Oh yes. Oh fuck, yes. You dirty animal, Viv. You dirty fucking dog.

'Ninety-six, respond or bring back the box.'

'Ninety-six,' says I into the two-way.

'The fuck you up to, Viv?'

'Go on, then.'

'Porchester Terrace. There's a phone number. Don't toot.'

'Ninety-six, roger.' Know that one, usually the airport. Who the fuck is this Roger? Way it works, they rent you the two-way. You get the work off it, pay them radio rent, covers the office, the controllers.

Next thing, Laura was on a kidney machine. Dialysis. Like Andropov, she said. Books in specific. I want that ninety-six, she told the controller. Oy oy, I thought at the time. What's this, a fat bird fancies me? Euch!

Wedges the thighs in the back. Portland AMI. Flash. Daddy's health insurance scheme. Got a dicky kidney, has to go on the machine three times a week.

Why you so fucking fat? I asked her.

And why are you so very ugly?

Now that's someone I can talk to.

It's not right, I said. People starving in Africa.

You don't give a damn about Africans.

You talking about my brothers, I said.

I'm having dialysis, she said. I'm not allowed to control my weight.

Oh yeah. Sure.

How many parts African do you think you are?

'Bout one in eight, I reckon.

I have Russian blood, she said. Russian. Italian. Australian. Greek. I'm a mongrel.

You act like one?

When I'm less fat.

So three times a week it was the hospital and back. Thought about her hooked up to the machine. Like me dad when he kicked it. Me mum, she was on at me to visit. Time I got there he was speechless. Give him a piece of my mind when she was resting. Just in case he could hear it, the cunt. The flesh, the metal, the tubes and needles, the rubber shoes squeaking on the polished floor. One of them pictures in the head which stands for something but you don't know what.

Sometimes you feel like a target. Different from a black cab cos of where they have the glass between them and the punters, I got this headrest, but there's a gap by the nape of my neck. Some of them, I feel like they're aiming at it. Laura give me that feeling.

Some things you let them happen in their own time. If you done a stretch you'd understand that. If you work the minicabs it's the same rule. Days you hit a rhythm – on the spot when a decent job's called, green lights all the way. (I had a run once, Peckham to Notting Hill, all greens; fourteen minutes.) Other days, you work your bollocks off keep getting poxy little local jobs, stuck behind every bus and grandmother on the road. So I waited for Laura to happen.

She has this thing, this true crime thing. Took me a while to see the pattern. This was in the dialysis bit.

'They're going to execute a man in California,' she said. 'Something Blithe.'

'Good luck to 'em,' I said. We was stuck in traffic up by Madame Tussauds.

'A kidnapper. Or so it seemed at first. He took these two boys – they were twins, I think. Then it became clear that he only wanted the car they were driving in which to do a robbery.'

'In which?'

'Avoids putting the preposition at the end of the sentence. It is correct English. Anyway, he shot both the twins, in their backs, the killings incidental to the car theft. It all happened at a drive-through restaurant. They were midway through their food. He shot them and then he finished off their cheeseburgers. "Coolly ate the remnants" – aren't journalists brilliant? He went and did his robbery. Later the same day, he was arrested on suspicion. One of the officers happened to be father to the boys. At the time of the arrest – for suspicion of the robbery – it was not known that the boys were dead. So when the officer mirandized Blithe, he had no idea that he was reading rights to the murderer of his sons. Can you imagine how he must have felt later?'

'They should top him,' I said.

'Wait. It gets better,' she said. 'The family history started to emerge during the trial. Cooked up by Blithe's defence lawyers, of course, but presumably on the basis of fact. Blithe's father was a child-beater. He incestuously raped Blithe's sisters. He – the father – was jailed for it. Blithe went in and out of institutions. Suicide attempts, self-mutilations. Once he stuck bits of a plastic spoon up his willy. They had to operate to clear the obstruction. At the appeal, the defence alleged that he was brain-damaged in the womb. Because his mother was an alcoholic.'

'They should fry him,' I said.

'I feel sorry for him,' Laura said. 'And I'm not the only one. Mother Teresa has written to the court, begging for clemency.'

'We've all had a childhood,' I said. 'It's no reason to go totalling kids. You want a car. Steal a fucking car.'

'He's got top billing on Death Row now. They asked him to order his last meal and he chose Kentucky fried chicken, pizza and jelly babies. Jelly babies!'

'You should meet some of these people,' I said. 'You wouldn't feel sorry for them. You'd do 'em with your bare hands.'

'I'm going to go and visit him,' she said. 'Before they kill him. Stage a protest.'

'Get off.'

'What else could he have done, the life he had?'

'That's bollocks,' I said.

The next week when I picked her up, she told me she'd been out there. Time she arrived he was with the fishes. So she goes to visit the cemetery where they put his charred remains. She only went and put jelly babies on the grave, for fuck sake. Or so she said.

There were flowers covering it, heaped for yards around it, she said. From all over America.

They need the Blithes, I said. You need the Blithes.

6

Lorry. Laura. Fatter than a London bus. So you couldn't find the places to fuck her even if you wanted, which I did not.

Used to get me to take her shopping. Door five at Harrods. Wait here, please. Had to keep moving to let the limos park up. Half a fucking hour. Buying the whole shop or what? This was after the dialysis. Asked her how it was – the kidneys. I was missing the easy business, see?

'What? Oh, that – cured. Miraculous, they said. Unprecedented.'

Cured? Well, whatever, I thought. Let it pass. Don't matter to me if it's true or not – probly shagging one of them doctors.

Then out she come, walking very fast through door five. Porter hesitates. Reckoned he might grab her. Swing open the passenger door. Shit. Fucking start, will you? Couple of blokes in aprons following her out the door. Limo tooting me, trying to swing over to the curb, let out the lady of the manor. Arabs, my guess. Diplomatic plates.

Laura, thump, into the front seat. Limo edging forward as I give it full welly. Clip the fucker's bumper. Door slams itself shut. Out into the traffic, off towards the V & A.

'You're no good at this,' I said to her.

'You don't know what I've got.' Phew, what a fucking stink.

'Go on, then.'

Hitched the skirt up over the knees, reached in there. 'Have a look.' Little glance she give me – kind of will Daddy be pleased? Started to pull this thing out, looked like she was pulling it out of her cunt. A fish's tail. Then pink salmon flesh, smoked, the skin cut away. A side of smoked salmon.

'Keep that thing off my plush.'

She cradled it like a baby. 'We need lemons. Have you got a cigarette? Let's go back, get some lemons. Yes, and pepper.'

How did I get involved with a fancy slag like her? That's what I'd like to know.

Yacking away, ten to the dozen, gone and got herself adrenalined-up all for a bit of salmon.

'We used to be taken to see the Father Christmas at Harrods. Lizzie and me. Margaret would take us. I don't think it ever occurred to Mummy. One year they had to fire the Father Christmas because he was interfering with the children. The euphemism makes the children sound like a telephone system or a radio network. You get your gift, you pay your price. Seemed to make sense. And then I read about this case the other day, the best I've seen in a long while. What better way to reassure a child than to tell him he was going to see Father Christmas? And what a time of year to choose. Easter would have been better. This one features pizza too. Pizza is the connection – you remember Blithe ordered pizza along with the jelly babies?

'Well, this one was called Barbra something-or-other. Barbra spelt that stupid way with an "ra" at the end instead of an "ara". There's something culpable in that alone. She commissioned two men to dispense with her son. He was four years old. What did he order, do you think, when they took him for pizza? Extra pepperoni? Who paid for the pizza? Did Barbra say, here's the money for the snuff and here's five bucks for the pizza?' Laura dug about in her handbag.

'Then into the Arizona desert, to a riverbed down a dirt track, miles from the highway. Little Jonathan. Four years old. Hold on—'

See what you get? Captive audience I am, stuck behind the wheel like a trapped animal, pinned behind it. The wedding guest syndrome, she called it, fuck knows why. She jumped out the car and raced across the road, coming back with cigarettes and lemons.

'So. Little Jonathan is dressed up in his favourite jumper – must get this salmon to a fridge – and his snakeskin cowboy boots. Thinking he was off to see Father Christmas at the local mall, the mall where his killers reported him to have been lost.

'The riverbed. Imagine the dry wind, fingers of cactus pointing to the guilty ones, a heat haze over the endless sand, the dust still drifting which marked the passage of the car to this point, this terrible sterile place. Two hundred pounds. That's all it cost. Three shots in the back of the head at point-blank range. A bargain for Barbra. Except it didn't take long for them to arrest her. She told the court that she had made a "bad judgment call" as if the whole episode had been no more than a game of tennis which she had refereed with insufficient care. I must stop smoking. Want one?'

'Nah.'

'What shall we do about Barbra Thing?'

'Must of been a nutter.'

'Let's say she wasn't. She told the court she was in her right mind.'

'I want that fish out of my motor,' I said to her. We was outside her gaff.

'Come and carve my smoked salmon for me. I have Chablis – two bottles.'

'Nah.' This was when she was still fat, right.

'She told the court that she had commissioned the

assassins to murder her son because she did not want him to grow up like his father, from whom – naturally enough – she was divorced. Kind. Joey and Barbra Kind, that was the name. Joey Kind was an alcoholic, an ex-junkie. Barbra couldn't face seeing her son turn into that. So kill him. Made perfectly good sense to her. Parenthood seems to destabilise people. They want to gas her. Her and the assassins. I've written to the judge. Sure you won't have some salmon? We could ask Lizzie to come and share it with us. That girl needs to eat.'

Then I never seen her for a couple of weeks. Disappeared, stopped calling the office saying, I want that nice ninety-six. I kept at it, driving ten hours a day, shagged the wife, serviced the motor, done the oil and pads meself but I had to take it in the garridge to get the power steering sorted. Kept thinking about her.

Why?

Fat slag.

She's not a fat slag.

She's nothing but a fat slag.

She's trying to tell you something, Viv.

But I don't know what the fuck she's on about.

Yes you do.

No I fucking don't.

It's just I can tell her things. Cos she tells me things. Cos she's out there where my head is.

You want to fuck her. Come on, mate, admit it.

Bollocks.

Driving around, I'd have these little chats with myself. Done my head in something horrible.

After that fortnight when she never booked me once, when she turned up she was thinner. I mean two stone thinner. Wearing clobber she must of nicked from Bond Street. New haircut. Red lipstick. Looked like a top-line tart. You could see the cheekbones. The waist. Nice pair of tits. In proportion. Nose was different. Beaky, like a hawk, narrow, sharp, strong. She had this sort of metallic glow to her, like a peacock.

'Well, look at Cinderella.'

'Eating is disgusting, don't you agree? I became bored with it so I stopped. Altogether. Mummy found me in the gym. I'd been on the step machine for ninety-five minutes. I think that's a record. In the hospital they made me sign this form saying they were allowed to feed me even if I refused to eat. I got on very well with the nurses – until mealtimes. Can we stop for some chocolate? I must, must must have chocolate. And then they were horrid. I would put the food – meat, two veg, a jelly with some sugary whipped cream blobbed on top – in envelopes. Big squidgy bookbags. Posted them to Mummy. Terrible trouble with stamps. There was a particularly stupid nurse who I persuaded to post the parcels for me. Can't have had much of a sense of smell. Look – here we are. Choc stop.

'Yum. Then they had me on a drip. Sucrose and saline. Well, I yanked that out of my arm and they plugged it in again. What right had they? I didn't want to be anchored to some machine. I wanted to float off. I found a way of switching the tubes so that all the products dripped into the mattress. Woke up soggy. They thought I was wetting the bed. Lot of stuff about regression to childhood. The consultant psychiatrist was pleased. They gave me a rubber sheet. I was expecting teddy bears at the end of the bed. Once they'd worked it out they strapped me – can you credit it? – to the bed, tubed up to the drip. Bastards!

'Not the most dignified position from which to receive visitors although hordes of people came to see me. Lizzie and Daddy and Margaret, of course. Plus the perennial tedium of Mummy. Even Billy showed up at one point.'

'Shut it, love.'

'Well, excuse me.'

'Slow down a bit.'

'If you don't want me to tell you about the nurse who fell

in love with me, I won't. Ernesto. Brazilian. Transsexual. Nor will I tell you about the time I turned blue at Daddy's birthday party. In Annabel's.'

'You told me that one before.'

'How I smuggled drugs into New York for Billy, inside me, in a Tampax. I won't tell you about that, either. Nor about the time when we were little and Lizzie tried to do me, as you would say, with the iron when I was asleep. Nor about Billy phoning up all the time wanting to have sex with me and Lizzie together. Nor about the side of smoked salmon Daddy gave me as a present, just because he loves me so much. I won't tell you any of these things. I'll just shut it, love.'

'It's all bollocks.'

'And I won't listen to you airing your guilt. Parading your petty villainy, your freak's circus of ridiculous half-cocked crimes—'

'That's enough.' I said to her. 'How do you expect me to know what the fuck to say with you making it up as you go along?' Then I said to her, I said, 'Stop acting like a cunt.'

'Oh, I'm a cunt now, am I? A gash. A muff. A snatch. A slit. A front bottom.'

'You what?'

'That's what the gays call it. The people you call shirt-lifters.'

Like a river broken its banks. Carrying all before her. Some of the debris was hers, some of it was mattresses and trees and corpses she picked up along the way, in flood. But it was entertainment. She was infectious with anything-goesness. Didn't give a shit what I thought of her. Started to feel like a padre. Hand out the fucking Aves.

I got loose. Told her stuff.

About Tel. Some of the others. That was a mistake, telling her about Edgware. I didn't see none of it coming.

Blinder than fuck knows.
All right, all right.
And you talk about stupidity.
Next thing, she only goes and commissions Edgware.

7

Then, it must of been a month later, I had a job with Laura when school was coming out in the afternoon. I never put it together till after. Not just coincidence. Made me slow down by the gates, cruise along. The way the mums glared at me, I felt like a dirty old man, eyeing up the schoolies. Some of 'em was hot 'n' all.

'Could you hurt a kid?' she asks me.

'Fuck off,' I said to her.

'No, I mean, if you had to. On a job.'

Not on your life.

'I thought you were a hard man, Viv,' she goes. 'Harder than a motherfucker.'

'Well, there's hard and there's sick,' says I. 'And a line between. Sometimes you lose the line, but kids? For fuck sake.'

Laura must have told them she was picking them up instead of their mum. Don't twelve-year-olds walk home theirselves? Fuck knows what she told them. They come over to the motor after a minute or two of her talking to them. Got in the back. Two little blonde girls. Ponytails, satchels, green uniforms, little ties, gym bags, white socks.

They don't say nothing, nor Laura neither. Even when I ask, where to? Just sit there. The kids start whispering in the back. Then Laura says to go to London Zoo.

We want to go home, say the girls.

Just drive, Laura says. Sweat, in little beads, on her upper lip. One hand picking at the nail of the other thumb, tearing the skin. Blood. She pushes down the lock button on her door. Central locking clicks them all down.

This man is a nice man, she says. His name is John. John is very, very nice. He is kinder than kind until he's cross and when he's cross he's very cross indeed so you be careful girls and we'll all have a lovely outing.

What's she playing at? Check the mirror. Kids whispering. Flat-chested little rich kids. Twelve years old. Well fed but pale.

When John gets angry he can be dangerous. Even when he's not angry. Isn't that right, John?

That's right, says I, and that's where it went wrong.

But we love you, girls. Oh yes, everything will be all right because Mummy and Daddy love you and so no one will hurt you. Not a soul.'

We want to go home, please.

What home? Laura pulls a bar of chocolate from her bag. The kids don't want none. Eat it, she goes, or Daddy will be angry.

They nibble at squares of chocolate.

Mind my plush.

Daddy likes to keep his car as clean as a whistle.

No flies.

Daddy is hard. A hard man.

She buys them pizza slices (that worries me) and Cokes at the zoo. Bit exposed for my liking. Fucking stinks anywhere near the animals. The lions – fuck me! The monkeys! Wouldn't catch me smelling like that.

Eat, eat, eat, says Laura. We want to fatten up our little girls, don't we, Daddy? Make them all round and puffy.

She was putting it back on as fast as what it come off. Face pudging out, nose slipping back into the blubber.

Nice plump little girls. Eat up or Daddy will be cr-oss. Singing the cr-oss on two notes.

Then the snake house, semi-darkness, holding hands in a chain, me at one end, Laura at the other.

Daddy is a reptile. Tread on him and he will wrap his coils around you, squeeze the very breath from your lungs. But you won't mind because it's Daddy-Oh. Oh Daddy-Oh. And Mummy is a fish.

She makes them get on their knees in the bird house. Pray to the birds. I'm bored of this. Might be weird, but who the fuck cares? I wanted to know if I was on waiting time. What do we do with the kids after the zoo, for example? So we go back to the motor.

Daddy wants to spank you now. You've been bad girls and he's going to spank you until you learn to be good. Every day, morning and night. And you'll thank him, because he's saving you.

In the motor it looked like she was asleep. On something again. Little white line of froth around her mouth, like the edge of the sea. Jerks to attention.

Put them in the boot, Daddy. I won't have this behaviour for a moment longer.

No, says I.

Spank them and put them in the boot.

Fuck off.

Daddy, that's a horrid word.

So we pull up at the light down the south end of Regent's Park. Old Bill in the motor next to us, looking across. I slip me hand behind the seat and open the back door, get rid of them. Kid grabs my hand, bites the thumb to buggery.

Then out they jump.

You'll be punished for this, my dears, yells Laura. I pull off swift but legal. Old Bill stays with the kids. Scarper up the Westway – a risk but gives you distance. Round the roundabout before White City, back in again on the Westway, duck down into Little Venice. Park up.

Is Daddy cross with me?

Daddy was very fucking cross with her.

GET THE FUCK OUT OF MY MOTOR. Look at this blood. What am I going to do?

Is Daddy going to punish me?

You must have times when it goes backwards. You do something, then you think about doing it but you already done it. I was pissed off. Didn't mean to clock her that hard, but I was provoked. I mean, was I provoked or what?

I had to jack in that motor, give it back to the HP sharpish. Shouldn't of never told her what a vicious cunt my old dad was. She knew I'd go along with it. Scheming little vixen. But there you are. Too much mouth on me, as usual.

Passing out on me, was that a bit of a melodrama, or what? Blood on me plush from her nose and my thumb. Half-masted, I was. Clocking a bird does that. Couldn't leave her there. Fuzz show up, fuck knows what she might tell them. Make me the villain, as usual. He kidnapped us, the mad bastard. And so on. But she's unconscious.

Sheer fucking folly. The oh-shit-I've-fucked-up-again feeling coming on. And I loved her, see? I do. Like a daughter.

Take her round the hospital, that's what I did.

Course you did, son.

Got her the medical attention.

Is that what you call it?

Fireman's-lifted her into casualty, dumped her on a bench. Nurses running out after me. Then they sectioned her. That was the first time. For her own protection.

What the fuck did they mean, mad? When I put all the pieces together, seems to me Laura done what she had to do. In the circumstances. But then I'm partial.

Then she started to lose weight fast.

More like a snake shedding its skin. Asked her what she was on cos the missus could do with losing a few pounds.

'My twin sister's on the mend,' she said.

'Wot sister?'

'Lizzie's getting better,' she said.

'Ninety-six, you picked up yet?'

'Ninety-six still waiting to pick up,' I said into the handset.

Some of the drivers, they got no patience. Me, I know how to wait. Live in the head, bide my time. Film production company on account. This Laura Blade. Back from the dead.

'Five five, you want number 60 Sinclair Road, picking up a Mister Chow. I still need one car on the shop. Someone give me a time on the shop.'

I swear, the skirts she wears, it's like a game. Opens her legs, knows full well I'm giving it a look.

There was one time she wasn't wearing no knickers. Honest. Thinks I'm part of a movie she's watching. But one day I'll come out the screen and give her a feel. See what she reckons on that.

Here she is now. Ticking, tick-ticking along in the black ankle boots with the stilettos. Good legs on her now, but she's tight-arsed, you can see it in the face. Knows what she wants but too frightened to ask. Some of the stuff I told her. I can see she loves it. Been trying to get her nerve up, ask me in. Take me out the movie.

Talk is cheap. Now she's getting ready to try a bit of dark for herself.

Act like a cunt, you get treated like a cunt, women taking the biscuit, which stands to reason.

Just how stupid people can be, you would not believe. You think, how could anyone be so stupid? What the fuck was all that about? But there's always someone who is that stupid.

*   *   *

She gets in the motor. In the back, which is unusual.

She invites me in, right? Her flat in Notting Hill. The parasite class – know what I mean? African masks in the hall. Primitive. Jungle music on the boom box. Moroccan hangings. Picture of this black geezer in the khazi, throat to belly, the muscles. These gels, all born in Wiltshire, think they come from Kingston, J.A.

Check the medicine cabinet (old habits die hard): Valium, Predictor kit, cap, Featherlights. What's this? Percoset? Nice. And a little bag of weed. Voltarol suppositories. Squidgy.

Used to be the front line, this street. Line's up in Tottenham now or down in Brixton. This place is full of the watchers, waiting for someone else to do something so they can be next to it. Adrenalin scavengers. Cunts. And all the ones like us, the ones with bottle, the animals, we can't afford to live here no more, just come back for carnival, when the watchers all fuck off to their country houses for the bank holiday. So they wonder where the action is. They need us to live, to make things happen so they can watch. But nothing happens. They need us, see? To make films about, write about, paint about, complain about, theorise about.

No, I am not being chippy. Fuck off.

Like that Blithe.

Quite right too. If you want a car, steal a fucking car. But they want to save the Blithes – this is the bit that gets me – they like the Blithes. Need them sitting there on Death Row, shitting themselves, ordering jelly babies. Blithe ain't no fucking use once he's dead. Well, is he?

'What's it all about, then, this movie of yours?'

'I suppose you could say it's about redemption. And rehabilitation. Sort of a bit like *Crime and Punishment* meets *Thelma and Louise* in Bermondsey. They've attached some talent to it and we're eighty per cent financed—'

'Yeah. What happens?'

'Well, once we have the money we start casting, finding locations, but we have to be a hundred and ten per cent financed before we can—'

'The story, for fuck's sake.'

'We're in a stage called development,' Laura said. 'Cappuccino or espresso?'

'No one knows what it's about?'

'There was this draft which we were all very excited about and then Mike – that's the writer – wouldn't make one or two changes which we felt had to be made.'

'So, who's the writer now?'

'Well, me, sort of. It's rather thrilling. But scary as well. I mean not exactly scary but – well – difficult. And you see we had this conference this morning and I'd put in a scene with a minicab driver and they liked it. They want me to go with it. The marketing people think it has legs. As an idea I mean—'

'And I don't?'

'Of course you do. As far as I can tell.' Listen to her. Tied up in knots. Magic.

'So you reckoned, offer Viv a shitload of money to tell it you like it is.'

'It's never going to be a shitload.'

'You owe me, love.' I said. 'Remember that Dean I told you about? Me and Dean done this doctor. To get his bag. Morphine. Diconal. Stuff like that. Called him out to this address in the middle of a council estate. This was up in the north-west. Doctor shows up, grubs about looking for the flat. I got a balaclava on, Dean has this scarf over his face. Over here, I shout. Dean comes up behind the doctor and grabs his bag. Dipstick won't let go. Shouting and screaming, You junkies won't get away with this, not this time, you filthy scum wasting a GP's time someone could be dying while I'm out here with you idiots. And so on. Unbelievable – no sense of proportion. Clock him one, Dean says, still trying to get the bag off of him. Fuck, it was cold. Started snowing just like Christmas. The doctor, he slips – ice on the pavement—'

'Perhaps I should explain the sort of thing we're looking for.'

'Dunno why I had the fear so bad. But there it is. Couldn't do nothing. Stood rooted. Fucking paralysed. Once the doc is on the deck, Dean gets the bag off him but the doc yanks the scarf, pulls it off his face. Trust Dean to choose his own fucking doctor to rumble. I'll have you for this, young Dean Torball, he goes. I'll see you in court, sonny. You've broken my arm and that's grievous bodily harm—'

'I think we could manage a weekly retainer. Say, five hundred pounds a week for a month.'

'When do you think I was born?'

'I'm not sure what you mean,' Laura said.

'It's not enough.'

'It's all there is.'

'It's not enough,' I said. 'What else you got to offer?'

'Like what?'

'Girl like you, become a writer this morning, you should be prepared to do anything to get your material, am I right?'

Then I said to her I said would she take her knickers off to get what she wanted and she said to me she said who says I'm wearing any? Oy Oy. Show me, I said to her and she said, would I lie to you, Viv? Course you would, doll, I said to myself. What is it about these fancy birds, I don't know, it's the way they look like they ain't never been given the full tour, only seen the front room of fuck, not the cellar and attic and the kitchen, makes you want to show 'em around. Naturally. They want it all right but they got the fear an all.

'What would you like me to do?'

'Listen,' I said. 'Dean says, Kill the fucker. Quiet. You got what it takes? Look at him, miserable piece of shit says he's going to bang us up. Fucking top him, Viv. He's not banging me up, I said, all bottle. Then I start seeing it, me doing him, opening up the doctor, caving his head in. Paralysed. Dean screaming, doctor on the ground holding his broken arm, Dean whacking him with the bag.

'I scarpered, Dean in pursuit, the doctor trying to come up off the deck like a boxer late in the count.'

'Perhaps we should go to the office—'

'We done the drugs. Got arrested later that night. Dean and me done the remand in a TC over Christmas. I done a runner and he went down for a couple of years.'

'TC?'

'Therapeutic Community. The psychology of it. That's what you got to understand.'

'It's very interesting and everything and I'm glad you didn't kill the doctor, but it's not what we're after.'

What is it you're after then, I asked her, and she give me the look. I told her she better tease it out of me. Then she said, if I treat you like a cunt will you act like a cunt?

Listen to it. Probably cost a hundred grand to educate her and that's what she come out with. It's a sin. Act like animals in the end, all of them, cos that's what we are. Parasites. Vampires. Scavengers. Well, what the fuck is a man supposed to do?

'You're the cunt around here,' I said to her. 'Don't even think about it.'

'You're a little boy, really, aren't you? Frightened of women the way you were frightened to hurt the doctor.'

'I'll fucking give you hurt,' I said.

Then she said, she honestly did, she said, do you want to hurt me, then? Pulling up the skirt and, true enough, no knickers and the muff looks slicked to me.

'Fuck off, will you?' I said.

She said, what is it the girls did to you made you so angry with us? Come over to me, sit on me lap. They love it, see?

Cunt frightening itself. Thinks it's safe, thinks we're having a lark. Was I provoked, or what?

Some of them need Blithe and some need Vivian. I like to provide a service. What God give you, no harm in putting it about.

'Don't do that,' Laura said. 'It hurts.'

'Shut the fuck up, why dontcha?'

It's tight.

She's yelping.

Slapped her about a bit – legs, arms – push her about, she's on the deck now. Then I get the knob in proper – feels like fresh turf. You get provoked into the brown. Loosen up a bit. Told her to squeeze.

'Like you was taking a shit.'

Couple of fingers in her mop. Heave a couple of inches into the muck. Screaming her bollocks off now, who says she wouldn't respond? Hands round the neck. Squeeze. Pa-tum. Pa-tum. Nice.

Can she breathe? Bit raspy, croaky. Whoops! Wriggling to breathe, is it? Which pushed her up against it.

'What we need now is something to put in your mouth.'

Grunt, rasp, croak.

'Nice black dick with a dribble of come on it. Keep you quiet.'

She liked that.

'Or another cunt.' Then it flopped open and I was in up to the root.

A bit still. Loosen off the hands.

Breathing hard now, trying not to move.

'Squeeze like I'm a big fat turd. Shit me out. Go on. Shit it.'

She made this sound like a horse kind of snorting and neighing all at once. Cunt's all astew, three fingers in there. Give her pubes a nice tugging, maul her tits. What a nice cup of tea we're having. Feel it boiling up, pushing herself on to me now. Her knees collapsed so I got my hips on her bum cheeks. Trying to make it disappear inside her? Trying to get it out? Trying to get it in further, don't know what she's doing. Hands on the throat again. Squeeze.

'Shit it.'

If I done her now I'd come like a goods train true enough. What's to stop me? Make her think I might. Consenting adults, see what happens, don't lose it, Viv. Hold on, son.

'Snotty little cunt like you,' I said. Croak, rasp, rattle. Rattle? Loosen off a bit. Might turn blue. 'Put you out of your misery.' Pa-tum. Pa-tum.

Brain her. Go on. With the lamp. Do it. Do it, Viv. For fuck sake.

With your hands, then, make less of a mess.

Think of mother. Slower.

Mother. Slower now. Slow down, let her push.

Push you out, back to the world, back up from the deep. Rattle, rasp, scream.

Then she come.

That was close. Then I threw me mix into it. Pump along. Squeezing me out.

I know she did. I felt it. A man knows these things.

'Now suck it clean.' Won't do it. Grab her hair, thick mane of hair. Make her. Wants to be made. They all do. All the same, these cunts.

Do her now, when she don't expect it. With that slab of marble, that ashtray. Or with the cushion. Go on. Just fucking do it. Make a mess of her. Fuck her up. Provoked.

The wounds in the hands. The weight of him – big fat bloke – pulling the nails through the palms of his hands. Making tears. Cunt-shaped wounds. Stay in the brown, Viv. In the brown sauce. The wrong fucking bloke.

Harder than a motherfucker, me. Slung like a pony. No flies.

Not a single one. Not me. Got her finger up me bum now, made me stiff. Slow it down now. Let go of her hair. I said, let go of it. Let her think, he's not making me any more. Can I do this now he's not making me? Wonder what it tastes like?

Lips drawn back as the mix comes. Splashing on her cheeks. On her throat. Where did she get them nasty weals on her neck from, I wonder? Like the sea, spray coming up off a wave, wind slapping it against your boatrace. We never took him down. They said he hung there till his fatness pulled the nails right through between his fingers. Big success up north. Turned his life around. Reckon we done him a favour. Taught him the value. Like resurrection, really. She could use that in the film.

But she done her research for one day, int she? Fucking right, she had. Fell asleep. Or made out she had. Always happy to provide a service, me. Specially when provoked. Funny feeling when I was getting dressed. Like there was this high wall behind me. These blokes up on the wall watching. Might jump down any minute. Always ready. About to jump. Dead already, all of them. Someone up there – is it a bit of gash? – she's going to push them down, roll them off the high wall, the minute I've forgotten they're there. I can feel it, the crump of the dead weight on my shoulders. Stumble under it. They land on me one after the other and I'm buried, me. The smell of them. The rot. That's a prison feeling.

I'll wash up later. Have a nice kip in the motor, park it up round the corner.

8

'Ninety-six, one on the shop or bell me, where you been?'
Bring me up short out of the reverie.

'Roger.' Where's the fucking handset? 'Roger.'

My dick hurts. She wanted to go back for lemons.
TIGHT.

'Roger what, ninety-six?'

'Bell you in ten, Tom.'

'Control to ninety-six out.'

Like a puzzle, me trying to put it together. Did she mean
the pieces to fit? Did she think about it like that?

Women, I mean, do they actually think? Not to say
they're stupid exactly. They have this other way of working
things out. Tied to the moon and the tides. Stuff blokes don't
reckon with.

And then maybe they're just a bunch of mad cunts.

'Nice ninety-six to control.'

'Rog, ninety-six. Dial me on your mobile.'

Punch in the little tune: 'What say, Tom?'

'That Edgware regular you used to do. He wants you.'

Shit.

'What d'you mean, Tom?'

'He asked for you specially,' says Tom. 'Birmingham wait
and return.'

Oh fuck. Haven't heard a squeak out of Edgware since—

The last time I done a job for Edgware things got right out of hand.

'Ninety-six, you want it, Viv?'

'Yeah.' Fuck it, I thought. 'Spose so.' Might as well be now as whenever. Better to take what's coming than live in fear of it every fucking day.

'Ninety-six to control.'

'Ninety-six, you what?'

'Leave a line in the book, willya?'

'Roger, ninety-six. Can do.'

Every job through the office gets logged, see? That way, anything happens, they can show them the book and it's just another job. But Edgware is special. He don't want nothing on the books if it don't go smooth. He puts up surety for the motor. The money is proper money and Edge, he knows his stuff. A true professional.

Can't talk about Edgware. Shouldn't anyway. But confession – the number of villains give themselves up, spill it all, you would not believe. Just pop in the local nick on an impulse and 'fess up. Bosh.

Filth rely on it, of course. Beats detection any day. Times you hear about it is when they done a bit of enthusiasm on the confessor, jog his memory. Media outrage 'n' that. But the 'fessors, they go in for it, in a way.

Must be tired or something.

It's the urge.

What if it is?

Don't be a cunt, Viv.

I want it all known, at least by someone.

Like a hunger. I can tell her stuff. Anyway, she tell anyone else who the fuck's going to believe it, a nutter like her?

Who you trying to fool, Viv?

Look, fuck off, why don't you?

Very, very tired.

Edgware never even belled after the last time. After a

week I thought, he's not going to do me. After a month I thought, I fucking wish he would bell me. I got used to the regular work, see. And the bonuses. The extra wedge.

But Laura fucked that up. Deserves whatever I give her and more besides.

Put her out of your head, son.

Call him Edgware. Nice and anonymous.

Have to tell someone about the last time.

Hold on a bit, son. Like with the bloke nailed to the train. So it's distant. Like a story.

Have to tell someone. Soon.

Very, very tired.

My theory? No such thing as a secret. Everyone has one person they trust, right? So they tell that one person. But logically speaking, that means soon enough we all know. Got to get the present and the past separate. Wish I could go home, wash up, have a nice shave and a cup of tea. Then a kip. I wish.

Edgware waits for no man. Be there in a minute.

You would never know him for what he is. Little runt of a bloke, balding with the Bobby Charlton wisps palmed across the top, try to hide the patch. Might be a milkman or a clerk. West Country accent. I done time with his brother. Shared a cell. Dead now. Reckon Edge done him. Brother had a lot of mouth on him. Told me stuff he never should of.

Now Edgware, he understands information. He likes to tell the bare bones. Not who give the orders, not who the target is neither. Just what he done between getting out the cab and getting back in. I get mileage plus risk money ranging from fifty quid to upwards of a grand. Always in tenners.

'All right, Viv?' He gets in the front with me. Least I can see what he's doing.

'Yes, mate.'

'Mind clocking off?' Which means we're off the books.

Bandit territory. If he does me, it's Laura to blame. But I give her the chance to fuck me up so I got what's coming. All from being too mouthy.

'Ninety-six to control.'

'Rog, Viv.'

'Turning it in now, Tom.'

'Drop the radio back when you can, ninety-six.' I get out the motor, take down the aerial which is on a magnetic base you stick on top of the boot. Stow it inside.

'Where to, boss?' I says to Edge.

'Birmingham, Vivian.' Edge has his little holdall and he's wearing his train-spotter's anorak.

'What gives?' I ask him.

'Do you know what they say, Vivian?'

'What's that, boss?'

'They say that sometimes you have to let things take their course.'

'Is that right?'

'I reckon it is, Vivian,' he goes. 'I reckon it is.'

'We got some sorting out to do,' says I.

'There's nothing to sort out,' he says.

'I had my reasons,' I says.

'It doesn't matter to me what reasons you had,' he goes. 'You know how to handle a motor.'

'True enough, boss.'

'More than that and you get confused.' Then he says, 'Stop the car.'

I pull up in a bus stop, hoping there'll be some punters about, thinking, he's going to do me now. It's come on top. The fear but the relief as well.

He gets out the front with his little holdall and then he gets in the back, right behind me.

I pull out into the traffic, thinking, any minute now.

Then I feel it against me neck.

'Ever seen that film *The Deerhunter*?' he asks.

'Twice,' says I.

'You remember the bit when de Niro tries to explain to the little punky bloke about life and death?'

'I remember.'

'He puts the shooter on him and he says to him "This is this".'

'Then,' says I, slowing down, 'then he pulls the trigger.'

'And what happens?'

'It's the blank chamber,' says I, the motor almost stopped, me whispering.

'It is, Vivian,' he goes. 'The blank chamber.'

'But the punk doesn't understand it cos he's never had the experience.'

'The blank chamber, Vivian,' says Edgware. 'You bear it in mind.'

Then he puts the shooter away. 'Wake me when we're on the motorway. I favour the M40. And please observe the speed limit.'

Discipline, see? He knows the value. Never done time. Never even been printed. A craftsman. That's what he says. Which he is.

With him behind me the fear gets worser and worser, me trying to keep my mind on the road. After twenty minutes he leans forward again so his mouth is by my ear and I can feel his breath on my cheek.

'Relax, Vivian,' he says. 'If I was going to do you I would have done it by now.'

'I been waiting.'

'Well, stop waiting,' he says.

I thought I was in the clear. But we had trouble in Birmingham. Bad trouble. Never got back till dawn.

All the way up I was thinking about fucking. Get close to being topped, you always end up thinking about fucking. I was thinking that fucking – in my case anyway – is very simple. Do what you want, get your knob wet, give her a thrill, shake her up a bit if that's what she's after. They all want that from me. Why?

Fancy birds see you as a bit of rough. They like a bit of a shock.

Parasites, really.

Don't like it with my own kind, see?

Nothing special to them, am I? Used to being knocked about. Nothing new. Don't care for them. Common as muck. Just want to get hitched up, have kids. Now with a shag I got control. But talk? Talk is different. I mean telling people stuff. Things that matter. Confession.

Gets right out of hand.

Never can tell when it's going to get the better of me. The desire. And that's how it is for most blokes with cunt. Can't overcome the impulse. Me, I can take it or leave it.

I could feel it coming all the way to Birmingham. Seventy miles an hour never helped. Couldn't talk to Edge. He won't have it.

Frankly, I never should of gone. It come on top something horrible.

Time I was back in town again I been up twenty-four hours and more. Look in on the wife. No. Can't lie there listening to her snore, waiting for the alarm to go.

You're all cunts. What's the point? All after something, aren'tcha? For nothing. Why don't you just fuck off and drop dead? Put Edgware on you, I will. Have him pay you a little visit. Then you'd understand about villainy. Leave off. Leave me alone, all of you. Scroungers.

Eight in the morning after Birmingham, haven't slept a fucking wink. Cabbing it over to Laura's flat.

This croaking noise. Choking, croaking, wheezing, sobbing. Delirious.

Must be a memory of fucking her, innit?

The voice in the motor, choking, wailing. Look in the

mirror – a face, light-skinned black geezer, bit of stubble, tears dripping down his cheeks. Looks like a kid.

Harder than a motherfucker, me. No flies. Treat me—

Motor's a right fucking mess. Have to garridge it. What about the two-way?

So I run past the office.

'What the fuck happened, Viv?'

'Leave off, Tom.'

Take the motor down the arches. Bit of luck, Tony's there. We bung it in the lock-up. Give him a wedge.

'You should watch yourself, Viv. Driving around in a motor looks like a fucking colander.'

Yeah, yeah. Black-cab it over to Laura's. Lean me forehead on the bell.

No reply. That's not so very fucking suprising, is it?

Once I buzzed all the bells to all the flats at once, someone let me in. Kick to the lock on her door, that done it in one.

Thank you.

Half asleep in the hall, in a T-shirt, staring at the floor. Oh fuck, I reckon she's got another bloke here. Fuck fuck fuck.

No. Worse. The what-the-fuck-are-you-doing-here-you're-not-part-of-my-life look. Followed by the don't-you-dare-touch-me-ever-again-you-animal look. But she let me in.

Come off it, Viv.

So I lie down on her bed. Fully dressed, mind. Lit a fag. She's standing over by the door. Then it started again. The croaking and choking. Sounded like a bird coming. I totally fucking lost it.

'My motor's knackered.'

Cunt didn't say nothing.

'Shot full of fucking holes.'

Stood there looking at me on the bed.

'Edgware done a job in Birmingham.'

'Edgware couldn't do a proper job on his own mother.'

'Whatever – shut the fuck up while I'm talking,' I said to her, I said. 'More vermin in there than what he anticipated. Someone must of snitched him up. He said when he went in, he said I'm going to adjust one bloke. Possibly two. Leave in ten minutes, he said, if I don't come out. Discipline. He has the discipline.'

'Get out of here.'

'I got nowhere to go, love.'

Listen to you.

'He comes out all right. Thirty seconds later. Running squatted down like I'm driving a helicopter. Couple of lads with shooters not far behind. I swung it round, he jump in the back, me heading straight for the lads, head down on the steering wheel. I got one of 'em, but the other keeps shooting.'

'Get off my bed.'

'Edgware is bleeding. We stop in a lay-by. Tie off his leg with the anorak. Lay him down. Gives me the address of his iffy doctor. That's me out of commission. That motor. They'll be looking. Where's the phone?'

Come on, Viv.

Fuck off.

Get with it, son.

Look, I had to hold her cos what's she gonna do, the state she's in, run off to the phone maybe, start calling the Old Bill, fuck knows. I was hugging her. Hugging her and restraining her. She wanted me there. She was glad to see me. She was my friend.

Yeah, yeah. That how you treat your friends?

'He'll live,' I says to her. Probably. Possibly. 'Iffy doctors can't always get blood. He lost a fair bit. It's not so much Edgware—'

Then I was blubbing again, like a kid. Loosen off on her, thinking maybe she might just hold me, like you would hold a kid who got hurt. Soon as I loosen off she tries to do a runner. I have to grab her again and that has me crying more cos she's my friend and she won't hold me.

Shut the fuck up, Viv. Just shut the fuck up for a minute. Bell Tony at the garridge. Spray it, flog it, junk it, burn it. The shit that's happened in that car.

I know I'm going to tell her, I can feel it, like when you get to the point when you've been giving it for a while and you get that extra bit stiffer and you know you're going to come. No way back. I'm going to tell her.

Get a fucking grip.

Laura goes loose inside my arms and I relax my grip.

'Please just go away,' Laura says.

When a person changes like that, how the fuck do you talk to them? I should go. I will go.

'You want stories from the dark side, I'll give you fucking stories. Remind you how you behave. Think I'm an animal, the stuff you done even animals never.'

Shut your big mouth.

Cry in front of a bird, look what happens. No fucking respect. Start trying to tell you what's what. Then you have to slap 'em. Show 'em what's what.

'You just remember what you done, then,' I goes. Certain tone of voice I have, women button it, even the mouthiest. Laura, she shut right up.

'When we cruised that school, all right? You says will I hurt a kid? Would I? Never. I tell you that's sick. Not hard. Sick. Got it?'

Nodded her head. Why the fuck can't she hold me in her arms instead of me holding on to her? Don't she understand nothing? What I done to make her scared? Just need a friend to talk to. So I'm not alone with it.

'What about them nieces come to visit you. Nieces, you said. Ten years old. Twins. Sweet kids, like to listen to your old records from the seventies. All back in fashion now. Try on your old platform shoes, the Afghan coat. Like no time passed at all, you said. Like I'm a teenager again. You and the twins down memory lane.'

'I need to go to the loo.'

'I'll watch.'

'If you must.'

She had a phone in there – must bell that garridge. I sat on the edge of the bath while she squatted.

'I can't,' she said. 'Not with you watching.' Doubled over, hiding herself in a crouch.

Get a little bit of what they want and then? Run away from themselves. A devil, that Vivian. Made me do the most disgusting things – like she never wanted it.

Crying now. It's catching. 'I don't want to see you.'

'Bollocks.'

'It hurts.' Sobbing on the bog. Pretty.

'You'll get used to it.'

'Please go away.'

Look what comes of showing a woman what she's afraid to want. Hark at it. What they don't want to see in theirselves. They decide it's yours. Wicked Vivian. The blackamoor with the filthy habits.

'You fucking wanted it.'

'You raped me.'

Can you fucking credit it? Make it up as they go along. People end up topping each other it's no surprise. I should string her up, show her what the word means. But I'm tired. Very, very tired.

'You came.'

Sob. Sob. No answer to that, is there?

'You ever come like that before?' Where the fuck am I going to go now?

'Bollocks, you have.'

Bell Tony, get that motor dealt with.

A bit of violence makes the world go round, the world go round. Did Edgware cross the river? Medicine cabinet.

Hope he did, the cunt. Harder than a motherfucker. No flies. Yeah, man. Medicine cabinet. Them Percosets.

'Nothing to be ashamed of, love.' Try that tack. Natural, like the beasts of the field. Do they? Don't know.

'Please – go – away.' What's she trying to do, crawl down the khazi backwards?

'Know what you are?'

'We're all stupid cunts, aren't we? What's the world like when everyone apart from you is a stupid cunt?'

'Don't you get funny with me, you little slag.'

Sitting watching her take a shit. Or trying to.

Time I gobbed some of them Percosets.

What a cunt Laura turned out to be. Who'd of thought it? Would you put up with that? Was I soft on her?

Don't you get funny with me, you slag, I said. Then she managed to lock me out the toilet when I went to get a fag to smoke with the opening flush from the pills.

Bosh – down came the door.

That's two doors today, Viv.

Must of got her on the nut as it come down. Doubled over the bathtub. Out cold, bum in the air, gave me half a mind to sink one into her. Wake her up sharpish. Accidental damage, I thought. Leave it at that. Had another look in the medicine cabinet.

Laura stirred. I felt her up a bit. It's just meat really and me dick was a snail. A snail crawling into a carcass. Nature's ugly. I leant the door up in the hallway.

I been walking aimlessly. Where am I?

Get yourself into gear, young Vivian.

Must sleep. When did you last sleep? Started 4 a.m. yesterday, that's twenty-nine hours. Well, fuck me.

Make a plan. Act. Then sleep. If Edgware croaks I got to clean his place up. Check. Get rid of that motor, get another one.

This stuff is serious, man, this Percoset thing. Warm rain.

Get off the street. Fuck knows what you look like. Make a list. Yeah. One, get a new motor. No: one, get rid of the other motor; two, visit Laura.

Three, score a bit of Charlie. No.

Three, sleep.

You could shag for hours on this stuff. If the mood took you. Could go back, teach a stupid slag a lesson. Just sit down a minute. Where am I?

Lancaster Gate.

Sort of crumpled just then. Pavement's warm. Amazing. Like a pillow and I'm the blanket.

Phone the iffy doctor. Did Edge cross the river?

Everyone getting hospitalised around me. Seems to happen.

Get off the fucking street, son.

Whoops, stick to the pavement. I never told her what I done though.

Oh fuck.

Here we go.

Woke up from dreaming I was inside. The smell of the other man's sweat. From fear. And piss. Always the same smell in the nick. Socks 'n' that.

Open up the eyes, have a butcher's. Too much light. Who left that on? Bed's too hard.

Fuck it, I'm nicked.

But why? Laura? Edgware? What day is it?

Stand up. Trousers fall down. No belt.

Bunch of cunts I associate with no wonder I get in trouble. Say it's drunk and disorderly.

Hang on to that.

Magristrate's court. Ticking off. Bit of a previous, this Vivian Black. Fell off the wagon, Your Honour. Fine me.

Dream on.

Accomplice. The Edgware thing. Could even try to stick it on me if Edge crossed over. Cunts.

Laura? Don't have the bottle to take the stand so it don't mean nothing. Unless.

Plead to assault, do a short stretch.

Could just spill it all, get some peace of mind. Act like a cunt you get treated like a cunt.

Don't you forget it.

9

Franz Marelli-Kreitznacht

My name, Franz; my mother Italian, from Trieste; my father German, from Dusseldorf, two PhDs – Munich (astrophysics), Zurich (comparative literature). I, for myself, tormented by self-loathing through childhood, plus ten years of mature self-pity. This is no joke.

I was lighting cameraman for new German films, also director of photography about to be. My father – this man should be dead by now – so great a love of cinema had; my mother believed the cinema was dead with Eisenstein. My analyst of the period – it was the seventies, so it was Helga – told to me to make films beyond my parents. Write the script. Easy to say.

Stockhausen, lotus-eating, Helga – that was the seventies. So many islands – like my mother's jewels in a blue satin box – but they had to come and my island spoil. No more solitude, but boatload after boatload of Milanese. Some pretty girls, some pretty boys, but animals in the mass. I made photographs of them, sexing on the beach, drunk, fighting in bars. Now this is all changed.

I was making development with a German director. This was the time of the new cinema. Everything was possible, even that I would to an understanding come with this father of mine, a brilliant man plus his prophetic shadow which all my days have darkened. Also, my mother, that my peace with her I might make.

Helga steered me, like the automatic pilot on the yacht what I then had, a guide who led me maybe where I was anyway going to go. Maybe.

My development was too much of the period. The first wave of German directors were all to Hollywood drifting. These floating pieces of America. One day they will drown. They get from me no lifeboat. A resentment which for five years we worked with – Helga and myself. Also later with Michaelis. My development was too much of MittelEuropa, before MittelEuropa again the focus became. Now they would probably make it but that is another life. No reason for you to understand: you are a pianist or a bicyclist or a cleaner of apartments, or a post-structuralist. If you are some kind of bigshot producer, I tell you, baby, you missed your chance. Kiss my ass. In the crack.

Pay attention, please. Always pay attention to the moment when things start to become unnatural. Listen to your body. The colon can speak to you. Also the muscles of the rectum and – girls – the vagina. The penis, this is clear, has its own grammar. This is no laughing matter. Listen to the shoulders. When you make a roll of the shoulders, like this, what do you hear? A snapping, crunching, clicking – not from nature. Not normal in nature but from a city life with bills and stress, money trouble, intimacy trouble, history unresolved. Let the body to speak. It stories has to tell. The throat: for many Germans the body stops at the neck. Also with the English. I have made a therapy for this. In an article in the newspaper they called me the plumber of the soul. When first I read this, I was bubbled with rage. A plumber! A dirty man with his hands always in the sewage. Cheating people, making bad work. Me, I am not this man. A higher plane I work. Thank you.

This was a tantrum, based on inability to conjoin with reality. Ha.

Michaelis (this was in the eighties and he was my potentiator – still is – steep Jungian, close friend) proposed to me the richness of the plumber analogy. So now I embrace this plumbing of the soul notion: to unblock in places many people prefer not to see a block, places many people will not acknowledge as places. To make my hand dirty in the faeces of humanity, in the dark places to search, to make maps of the psyche's septic tank.

And still the perverts they come for champagne enemas. I make this to pay for the ones who need help. Also equipment. Also, my mother's hospital care. I will never let the nuns have her. Carmelite bitches from Hell.

Never, *never*, underestimate the toxicity of emotions blocked up, unflushed. Never! Honour this rule and you will recover. This my promise is.

How it started was with Helga. She had her own agenda, but did she own her stuff? This woman I made a calculation which now it does not matter. One time each week in her bureau, then also telephone consultations; nine years the fee always rising each September. Helga cost me the price of a new BMW. Seven series. Aggregate. And she asks me to donate my island house for an institut, the Institut of Cycladic Healing.

But I thank you, dear Helga – I beat you with a stick and then I thank you – for this is now my institut. Also, the lawyers I thank. I invite you all to my next open day. Take a boat from Piraeus, bring a friend. I will tell you one thing of the Greeks in parenthesis: they make plumbing the worst outside Africa. The pipes are so that if you put the paper after you wipe (I hope you wipe) then the drain it blocks. Beautiful.

At my Institut we have big pipes, imported from Germany. Every facility has an inspection shelf – my clients must all be aware of their stools – and two-speed flush. One day this Helga I must flush away from my spirit.

I have an international referral system, built up over fifteen years, a winter institute in Florida – Captiva Island – and consulting rooms in London.

OK, my *métier* I have found. Still, they should have made that film.

Helga? Discredited. Washed up. A counterfeiter. A person of no account. You know she was not even qualified?

No, no, no: I can show you my certificates. Every year for three months I take a course – to embrace the whole person you must be electic. Also, if possible, a visionary. Homoeopathy, Kleinian, Archetypal, Bly, Rolffing, EST, Tavistock, Lacanian, Psychosynthesis of Assagioli, Aromatics, psychopharmacology, even the mad progenitor and acquaintance of my father – may his soul circle in hell for ever – Sigmund Freud (also, the daughter Anna, who was less crazy than the father). Thank you. It is an achievement and each day a new beginning is. (Freud in hell, not my father.)

Laura Blade was referred to me by Michaelis. A textbook case. By which I do not mean standard, or regular, or even predictable. Only that certain principles were clarified.

OK, maybe not clarified yet.

The entire burden was focused upon an obsession with flight. In many ways this was spiritual – redolent of so much and she was not stupid. Would that she had been a little more stupid and I less blind. This flying fixation was an umbrella (once she was Mary Poppins, a nanny of popular British myth) under which she had concealed everything else. One woman should not so much power have. Helga, Laura, Maria; also my mother. How do these kind of women seek me out? Thank you, Michaelis, for insisting that I seek them.

There are people coming to my Institut you would like to meet. The ones we used to call Prince people. Now these people, since the L.A. riots, are too afraid to go out and buy a newspaper. I am not a thrower of names or a dropper of weight but only a man beset by certain ironies, ironies I have struggled to embrace, to laugh, to get myself a good feeling. The affluent, the fairly famous – not with a visitor's file like the Betty Ford, but not so far to go. These people, they come to me for salvation. Fifteen years ago they would not take my calls, nor even those of my agent. Well, well. How many calls can you take in a day? They get back to me now, and I speak to them. Unless I am in conference. Which mostly I am.

I have the sound, healthy mind-body-emotion-spirit, full being in harness of godness. They have the film deals and the options, the stress of the fourth writer and the tenth rewrite and the distributor pulling the money; they have the little problem with the diet pills or the nerves breaking or sometimes the heart breaking. In this I believe. It can be broken, easy. Only for some can it be mended. This is harsh. With some of them I would like to compare my Swiss bank balance.

We make an exchange. For these people my Institut is expensive, and slow. You think I a snob am? I dive with the fishes, also lie down with the lamb. There is sometimes work with animals: goats, cats, dogs and, when we are blessed with calm, dolphins.

Again, misunderstanding from the islanders, also the press. This is the rationale for my open day. The islanders will never understand, even though they now respect. One of them, a bus driver, had a nervous collapse. With him I did some work. A simple man, even a good man, but a bad driver of buses. You must know your power, also your weakness. Accept the balance of account, totally, and adapt your aspiring to this balance. Then you will get a good shake. This man, he came to understand that he was not a driver of buses. I taught him how to grieve for this, also for the tourist what he overran. Now he runs a bar in the port. Pays for his son to go to college in America – law school. I love these peasants, each of them working towards a style of living that has destroyed the people who visit their island to seek my help. One or two of the older ones still make gardens in the valley, grow things, use the land. These men I ask to drink a glass of the good wine on the lower terrace at day's end. One will bring honey, another spinach, one cheese of a goat. Flowers, maybe. These ones have something to teach but no language with which to articulate their knowledge. I make translations. So.

When the body is blocked the mind is never far behind. Also, vice versa. The colon. Also, liver and kidneys. Many people come to my Institut paying full attention to feelings, listening to themselves feel bad about themselves. This I know. But how many to the body listen? What is the heart doing today, how does the breath draw? Exhale – psyche equals breath, this you know – why is there this stooping, or the shoulders always pulled up to bury the neck?

So, for the first week, no talk outside the group, also often no talk inside the group. Listen to the cicadas, the wind – now we have phone lines it howls – and the waves on the rocks below the Institut. What Helga understood about my island house is that here is a full feeling of otherness which we can maybe use to change the direction a person's life is taking. She comes here for the first time and tells me what I know only too well from a decade of summers.

'But why have you not changed, Franz?'

'You think I have not changed?' I said.

'What do you think?' Classic Helga undermine! Refusing to affirm sense of undermine, leaving subject dangling above new hole, or even let subject fall into new hole, break a few bones. Beautiful.

If I was slow to change, Helga was the handbrake which needed to be released. One time – by this stage we had most of our conversations via our lawyers – she telephoned me.

'Haven't I suffered enough?' she began.

'I cannot talk to you,' I said. Legal instructions, also psychic protection.

'I am not your mother, Franz,' she said. 'I was not the one to deny you.'

'There is nothing I can say to you.'

'I am going to give you the house, Franz,' she said. 'You cannot heal yourself by destroying me.'

Right now that statement has a bad echo. The same thing that I said to Laura.

But is it true? With Helga, it worked out pretty good for me. But with Laura I must wait to see. My life is not a china shop. Some things must be broken. Broken and thrown.

'I give you the house,' she said.

An expensive remark. Recorded. My house. All mine.

Why did I let her have it in the first place? I do not wish to pursue this line of enquiry. In my siege mentality, by Laura besieged, I must be simple to survive.

Now we will do stretches.

Extend a muscle, you also open a vista in the mind, a door in the heart. Try to learn. There is no one else to be in your body for you. Some of the bodies I would like to be in, for sure. Some I get in. Not always so ethical, but I write the code. Things sometimes become a little ensnared; myself also.

But there is always the weekly counter-transference group: drain down the system, flush it through. This year, for reasons which will become clear to you, we lost sight of those groups.

For the patients, I will tolerate no nooky, not patient on patient (or let us say guest on guest). Sometimes I use the sex tool to bring a person to her body. Or his. This we do

not talk about so much. Many sound therapies are open to
misinterpretation.

Precedent: tantric yoga. Thank you.

For myself, this duty a pleasure can be. Do not laugh. I
make healings. Did Zeus leave the mortals alone? How else
would there have been an Achilles, a Helen? Where did this
correctness get anyone?

But somehow the dynamics went wrong. This is evident.
Why would I blame myself? Maria was foolish. Laura is
dangerous. A new negative mother with whom I have
chosen to dance a symbiosis. It is something from which I
can learn. Do not try to place the fault at my door. Most of
all the patients learn. They get the money's value (often the
medical insurance pays . . . check it out). They are changed,
renewed, or at least other. Also myself. There is no wisdom,
no ritual possibility which I will not attempt to include.
Judge at your peril.

There has been a conspiracy. You may think I am paranoid, but the women have schemed against me, always the
women, these witches of Hecate putting themselves in my
way. They have tried to break me. Dream on, ladies. After
Helga, I am tempered. Still, I have some pretty serious
patching up to make on myself. Any minute now, the
last patient goes. I close for the winter – go to Florida.
In the spring, we have new whitewash, new clients, new
conditions to heal. It will be OK in some kind of way, even
if Laura is with me still.

Out there in the conurbations the stew of pathology
always spits out new victims. A few mistakes cannot ruin
me. There will always be more hurt than I have time to
heal. That's how He must feel.

They lie to me. If only they were less in need of untruth.
Most I see through, some it is harder to read, some are just
opaque, a blackness – only through the body can you help
this type. They open the mouth, out comes the shit. Laura

Blade was one of these. And sometimes the body too is opaque, a blackness in the core of the body from out of which creatures crawl, parasites. I tried to make her give birth to this blackness, to the creatures harboured by the blackness. But I did not expect her creatures to invade my Institut.

Bad judgment.

Or compassion fatigue? Could be. Darkness, we like to call it by some other name, for we live by light. I watch thanatos, down below the house, on the rocks, the water, the cove where the fisherman using explosives to make a catch up himself blew on his way out to the channel.

I am a little shook up. I have not been able to leave my apartments in the Institut for one week. Clearing up after the women. OK, there is a problem a little beyond group dynamics.

I listen to my body but he will not speak to me. Bowel movements pretty much in disarray: Monday – nothing; Tuesday – figs, loose noxious slop, no definition; Wednesday – good solid cylinder with thinned tail, odour almost sweet, compact, chestnut brown (no more troubles, I think); Thursday – black water splatters the bowl, enraged emission, stench of death; Friday – constipated.

10

My father preached the value of systematic honesty. By this he meant scientific accuracy of observation. My mother, the rigours of the confessional espoused, searching the soul for sin. She was married more to the church than to my father. She sought his failings and mine with twin spotlights of guilt and shame. Both one then the other of these forebears I have fought against. Now I incorporate both, to make the eclectic synthesis.

Even if she will not speak to me, Laura can perform on me full colonic irrigation before they close down the equipment for the winter. Ripeness is all.

Thank you.

The figs are split and dried on the branch where the boy was too lazy to reach up. Below my window I can almost reach down and pick. But I leave the black seeds to spill in the wind. I should have plucked and eaten Laura before she had a chance to spill.

You should watch the marketing video for the Institut of Cycladic Healing, check out what kind of a place I have. Thirty-five-millimetre. There is the original house which I built in the seventies when my father gave me the Bosch shares. The architect followed the line of the hill, flowing with the steeply sloped terrain of the island, working with the flat terraces made by stone-walling the hillsides.

We tried to retain the vegetable character of each terrace

as much as possible. On the terrace of wild herbs we make the kitchen. There was a cactus forest inside which we built the water cisterns. On each terrace we made a different type of living space. The central tower, surrounded by figs, is my private quarters. We made stone steps, whitewashed, connecting the terraces, plus long white stairways down to the rocks, to the beach, the dock, to the place for garbage. From the other side of the bay you see these stairways like white snakes basking on the rocks.

And when I raised the money to build the Institut on the new hectares, I followed the same principles, building up the hill, each terrace a living space for one resident with bedroom, bathroom – big pipes, as I say, use as much paper as you like – also a little outside place to make meditations, olive tree, fig, vine, screen of bamboo for privacy. Plus we have cypress trees, eucalyptus, and one palm tree over the terrace outside the main group room. And, of course, gerania all over, rich red against the deep blue of the shutters and the white of the walls.

Space for twenty-five residents. I made a beautiful thing. Also, I made one room which I always keep empty. A votive place. Helga's room, sometimes; also the room of my mother, my father. This room is always empty, please understand, for I must have a place to store my spectres.

Yes. Yes, indeed.

The tower is private. Maybe I tell you later. You know Yeats? I do not understand the feeling of inexplicable longing which comes over me when I see an aeroplane pass overhead too high in the sky for me to hear the engines. Possible that this is a Maria thing. Maybe also to do with looking back over a summer from the autumn perspective. Who knows?

For now I cannot look directly into the inferno. I must look further back, to my new beginning.

The island at the time of Helga's attempt to rob me of my

house was becoming overrun by rascals. English, Germans and Milanese Italians came to get drunk, also to sex; usually too fuck-drunk to sex. Also violent. Cheap people in campsites, beer-drinking, shouting into the quiet night, vomiting every which where. This was the bad business of louts exposed to Dionysian possibles.

It was partly because of this that I began to concede to Helga's submissions. I will make another place, I was thinking, away from all this flotsam of humanity rutting under mosquitoes biting. Let Helga witness the last chapter of the Paradise-ruination. Partly, but no more than a part, for so much was to do with my incapacity to refuse the request of a proto-mother on a Helga-scale. Alien. Bitch. Also, harridan, Medusa, Cybele making the men the testicles for to chop. But why?

If on your back you carry the shame of mother also father also analyst, you will always capitulate to these people and to people like them.

No power. This I have lived through. I know it.

You want another principle? Start to say no. No No No. Put this word in your mouth each morning, spit it out all day long.

Picture a peasant village transformed into bars, dirty sleeping rooms to rent, discotheques damn-everywhere, boys also sleeping on the roofs in the village, sometimes they roll off when drunk, one or two die even, but not enough. A rabble of sun-crazy rapscallions and their concubines rampaging under the starlit vault of heaven, looking to the price list and curvature of the buttocks, never up to the sky in wonder.

He must have felt the same when He overturned the tables of the money-lenders. But I did not want to make a riot – not like my friend who was driven to distraction by the noise pollution of the bar by his house on the beach (do not on sand build, some Bible things are true). At zero-one-hundred hours he rushed into the place, ripped the speakers from the wall, also upon them stomped, then threw the amplifiers to the ground. A beautiful gesture, but expensive. When is beauty ever cheap? Once upon a time on this island: that was then.

It was late spring when Laura arrived. Maybe middle of May. Then two gentlemen on their way to Mykonos who come for colonics, quick visit. A disgraced French government official, nerves all broken up from sexing the first under-secretary of the Swedish embassy in Rio – boys together in the broom cupboard.

A week later the couple arrive from Boston, husband and wife team of binge drinkers in their forties, textbook co-dependents. An eating disorder, a depressive, plus three regulars on the world tour of therapeutic institutions, all who have made a lifestyle of victimhood, identifying in each locale a new disorder which they can take to the next port of healing. Harry, for example, arrived as an overeater and departed as a battered child; next year he will be a depressive and the year after that perhaps an alcoholic. With these, the ones I call the perennial patients, denial has become a complex and sustaining theology.

I will have nothing said against these regulars. They are walking their own purgatory and we must help them on their way. They need the industry and by God the industry needs them.

Not so easy to keep your vision pure, nor your body.

In this world of empty churches the body is the only temple (even so on this island alone there three hundred and sixty churches are, one for every three full-time islanders).

But I say, worship your own temple.

Resistance and denial coupled to arrest Laura's recovery. When she arrived, I gave her the Silence-in-Group T-shirt, put her on a daily swim across the bay, with the snorkel – teach her to look down into the deep – also the churches hike across the mountain.

I told her, observe your stool, make notes. What they had her on in the hospital in London, Haldol, also Largactil, made her face bloated, made her talk louder than necessary.

She was fat, with wobble of the buttock. I turn away from this, like bad poetry: avert the gaze. A strange girl, maybe once beautiful, I thought. For the transformations I was not prepared.

A history I try to make. Everything was riddled with contradictions. Bulimia was evident. The rest I could not see. She repeated the story again and again of Icarus into which she had transposed herself. 'I have had a crash landing,' she said over and over. Her mantra.

Literal meaning of tragedy? Goat-song. Thank you. So the tragedy of the Greeks was from a ritual sacrifice. Maybe goat-scream. Also, goat-death-rattle. I will quote you from Yannis Ritsos on this.

This place is mine, OK? I conduct things how I wish. What do you know about it? Tell me that. Tell me that if you can. They are brutes, these people I have to work with – animals. The Americans and the Eurotrash, each as bad as the other.

Maria was not a trash. Maria, my strong, strange baby. My assistant director. Child of my heart.

The day-to-day was wearing me down. The Boston couple, the ones who drink in a binge, were accusing each other of secret indulgence. The Frenchman tried to adjudicate. The common language was German. None of them spoke it well. Some kind of a mess. I needed two Marias for these groups.

This was all in the early part of May, when my nativity approached. When the nights were still cool and the rush of the midsummer was still to come. Before everything was ruined.

The summer of my half-century. Halfway through; maybe much more than halfway through. We make a little party in the Upper Valley. Michaelis came from London, some Greeks, French, Austrian and German friends from the island. Maria was the only one from the Institut.

There had been organisations; plotting and much busy-bodying.

I must say I wish to propose a society – a microcosmos – in which it is possible to fully control events and behaviours, to stop people acting on my behalf without prior consultation. In my republic there would be no *laissez-faire*. Perhaps not a republic, maybe a principality.

A surprise party – for myself, this is some kind of rape. Turn your back on people for just one moment, all begins to splinter, to fall apart. Intolerable. You will understand why I must keep a watch on everyone.

How must He feel?

Pretty much given up on the whole circus. Cutting His losses.

Kyrie Eleison.

When I arrived at the party for my fiftieth birthday – at a hunting lodge in the high valley – I found the people I expected. Then, at sunset, I saw them unpacking some old lady from a jeep.

My mother! In a wheelchair, come to wish me a happy birthday, calling me Antonello. She and my father always fought over my nationality; she would still reclaim me for Italy if she could. They none of them understand that I made this island a place for myself to avoid just such a scenario. These fuckpigs, do they understand nothing?

My mother was weeping. Also myself. She told me how she prayed for my eternal soul all through Lent. No wonder I was feeling so rough. She believes I have become a follower of Dionysus – they showed her cuttings about the Institut.

She imagines me burning in Hell. I send her Nietzsche to read, so she might understand. But she sees the word anti-Christ. Straight to the incinerator. I pay to keep this woman alive, can you believe, thousands of marks (millions of lire) per month.

We took a glass of champagne together while I attempted to compose myself. Not much good – tightness in the shoulders, bowel in spasm, also anxious perspiration in the genital zone. Every time she addressed me as Antonello I experienced this blush of the whole body from scalp to thigh. I caught Michaelis – you will recall this man is supposed to be my therapist – eyeing me across the room. Next I expected him to start taking notes. Is there no peace? Is there not someplace where I do not have to be watched?

Ya, ya. I know. I know. But that is different.

Once I had settled my arrhythmia, made some deep breaths and recited to myself from *The Art of War*, they brought in my father.

This was three kilometres beyond too much. Pappi on his Zimmer frame, old head like a football, ears like an elephant. The sparkling stones of his eyes still lit up and crazed. (When I was a boy, I believed that his eyes could cut me, as a diamond would cut.) The childish desire to run away almost overwhelmed me. I was stuck to the very spot.

I would rather they had brought Helga to my island, plus the collector of taxes and the Archangel Gabriel to sit in judgment upon my foetid soul. Mammi was muttering about confession – when did I last? Who was the priest? Had I forgotten the bliss of absolution?

At the start of his studies, when he was a young man, Pappi was at Cambridge. He would go to the tutorials of Wittgenstein. With many of his pupils this Wittgenstein asked that they retreat from philosophy into working with the hands. Pappi fell for this preposterous crusade and for a brief period of his young life professed himself a desire to become a plumber.

Fact: Wittgenstein desired an improvement in college plumbing – never was there an adequate supply of hot water for to do the washing up. Pappi, Ludwig thought, might champion the cause. Pappi was more interested in why his master had put all ethical considerations beyond the boundary of philosophic thought. Like all young ones, he wished for a definition of the good, also the bad. Ludwig would not speak to him of this and so when of the dirt on the hands he tired to Munich Pappi went, for to study astrophysics.

When some fool sends Pappi cuttings from the Institut in which I am described as plumber of the soul, he thinks all is well between him and the shade of Ludwig. My son, the plumber what I never was. Always he addresses me like this. The pleasure in this is exclusively my father's, unless we predicate an afterlife in which Ludwig listens. But Ludwig would disapprove of an afterlife, even a predicated one. So.

Less a birthday party than a scene of primal trauma washed down with French champagne. Pappi and Mammi would not speak to each other, while Michaelis was voluble with both of them. He was making espionage upon my childhood.

You might say – I said it to myself that night – that it is as much the duty of the analyst to betray as to be loyal to the subject.

The subject passed his breaking point, walked out of his own birthday party up into the hills under an almost full moon, wishing he could observe the scene from the outide. For preference, through the viewfinder of a camera.

I reached the ridge and looked down to the other side of the island. A big herd of goats approached. Their little bells recalled to my mind the church bells of childhood, with Mammi and Pappi fighting over whether Antonello/Franz should go to Mass. As the animals shoved past me, I let my hands pass over the pelt of each. Then I sat and watched the goats swirl down the hillside, pausing to pluck and grub, following some fuck-knows plan of their own.

I was experiencing the tragic vision of life which seemed to me to lie somewhere out in the Aegean vastness. The black shadowy shapes of distant islands stood out from the silvered surface of the sea under moonlight and the two nearest islands were for me the ghosts, not of my father and mother, but of some mother and father I desired but could never have. I was angry that it had taken fifty years for me the understanding that whatever the force of my desire, it would never be fulfilled.

I was in a form of dead time, my limbs heavy and my thought slow. I began to weep.

From this point the cartography of my summer was turned upside down. The pattern began to break up, events unfolding as randomly as the passage of the goats down the hill. I have yet to find the new pattern.

Next day I went out in the powerful boat with Michaelis. Tried to put Humpty Dumpty together again. Before the repairs were complete, he made conversations with two Swedish girls on the beach and offered them a lift back to the port.

The one called Inga lay naked on the back of the boat, on her stomach, legs apart. I noticed her rectum was kind of frilly, like a cabbage or a flower. Michaelis also saw this. I could not make him speak of anything but this frilliness. He stayed on the island two extra days to chase the Swedish cabbage. I was in full trauma of relived childhood – betwixt the Catholic church and the whereof/thereof, the iron fist of the father and the suffocating dugs of the mother – and this Michaelis of mine talked only of his quest for the dark passage of Inga.

'Do you think it has teeth, Franz?'

'A cabbage with teeth?'

'*Rectum denticulata*,' he said. 'You could write a paper about it.'

He did not succeed with Inga. A case of bad attitude, I would say.

The world goes like this, ladies, do not be offenced.

Michaelis left me with a promise that more clients would soon arrive from his London practice – 'a couple of tough ones. Good for the full eight weeks and both on medical insurance. Should help your cash flow.' Michaelis's biggest betrayal was that he gave me no warning about Laura, the snake he had already delivered into my garden.

The boat which took Mammi and Pappi away – oh happy vessel – brought some new guests to the island. A Texan bulimic, a junkie French heiress and a once-Robert-Bly-acolyte with a new sex change, 'he' having a few problems adapting to the 'she'.

Maria – dark keeper of my heart – lived in a house directly across the bay from the Institut. A few rooms and a terrace in the foothills behind the beach.

Why should I not have kept an eye on her? This was a management duty. A key member of staff. I was watching out for the well-being of the Institut.

Also, I feared she was a slut and a slut I could not have populating my imagination so much of the time. Always for me my mother wished a girl of pure virtue; my father wished merely a girl of pure blood. I had to discover the purities of Maria before with her my body, also my reputation and my Institut, I could share. Information is power. Bad information is a virus. Watch how it spreads.

In my tower of technology, one telescopic lens always points towards the house of Maria, taking pictures on a time-phase programme. Just to be sure. And – yes, OK – sometimes I think it would be good to watch her disporting with a

Gustav or a Jimmy, a Jenny or a Dagmar. You must not speak of this. You keep your part of this deal, I will show you things for sure you will like to see.

There is a wider issue of belief. If I take pleasure only from observation of the therapeutic process and not from the process itself, then I am maybe just a washed-up thing and should devote myself to some other profession. We can pursue this later. For the moment I have bills to pay, a business to run.

You wish to mount the arguments against this observation tower of mine, hold your horse until you can see how this thing unfolded. So, they have the youth, also the beauty on their side. But I have the truth, also the equipment. The facts: you cannot dispute the recorded facts.

That I failed to record one of the important facts – I curse myself for this. No need for you to join in. I cannot record everything. There is a limit to my equipment. I try to keep a track of Maria, sure. But when she was working one hour in the group, the next with the sex-change, popping in on the Texan bulimic – how can I make a tape between all the different locations while I myself was running a group? Next year – if there is a next year – I will have a technician, someone I can trust, someone to track the movements of . . . well, it will not be Maria, but whoever the Maria of next year . . . if there is a next year . . . but who can I trust?

I observed the ending of a group, the Boston alcoholics beating cushions with baseball bats. The cushions were the children of these alcoholics. The French heiress junkie – Brigitte – was weeping from witnessing this rage, also maybe as a result of her detoxification programme. I hoped maybe she would find a rage of her own but she needed more time. The diplomat I have given up on but he pays cash, so he stays. He sat in a corner playing with a baseball bat, fingered it like it was the cock of some street-boy. These people make me sick. Yet my mind is open even when the viscera revile.

I climbed the stairs of the tower, entered my bunker of full elevation. Lucky for me, monitor B was to Laura's hut in the Institut tuned.

Do you understand the thrill? To have secret knowledge of another and for the other not to know you know. I watched her in conversation with Maria.

Would you the opportunity pass up? To fly on the wall of your belovered as he or she talks to a confidant(e)?

You must understand this. I know what Maria does. Also, I do not know what she does. Both of us, we choose knowledge and ignorance of the other to suit the time of day.

Laura – how it turned out I should have put a stake through her heart. Save a lot of trouble. But I wanted to plumb the depths beyond her surface pathologies: sink my hands in the mud and miasma of her soul, up to my elbows. As with Helga, I have yet to learn to turn away. The attraction of that which will only hurt me is still too great.

I switched the monitor to watch Brigitte play with herself on her bed. She was reading the *Fear and Trembling* of Kierkegaard – strange things some people choose for to turn on. The sex-change boy I saw inspecting his new breasts before the mirror, weeping at the girl he had become.

I switched back the monitor to the camera concealed in the ceiling of Laura's room.

'I only feel it would be unfair not to warn you,' Laura was saying.

Of what?

After a fortnight in the Institut, Laura Blade had changed. Loss of weight, sure. No drugs, sure. Body clean, also fit from swimming and hiking. She began to look like a woman, instead of a piece of dead fish.

'After all, Maria, you are very attractive,' Laura said.

'We have a professional relationship.'

'The oldest profession,' Laura said.

'I don't understand,' Maria said. Myself neither.

'I've done it myself,' Laura said. 'I even enjoyed it sometimes. Paying for it liberates them. Loosens them up a treat.'

Laura thought she was in some kind of priapic play-pen with therapeutic side-orders. Thought she would be indulged by Franz Marelli-Kreitznacht. Think again, young one.

'He has never touched me,' Maria said. True. True.

'He doesn't need to,' Laura said. 'I know about these things. One day soon I'll prove it to you.'

At this point, yes, I should have Laura from the Institut slung or cleaned up my own act. For there is a type of person – a type of vulnerable – which seeks out by X-ray the weakness in others. To underestimate the acuity of such a vulnerable one, this is a form of failure to observe, plus pride. As one who so much time observing spends I should – fuck knows – have recognised the threat.

But no.

Laura was not just thinner, she was sharper. Rapid movements of the head to notice all what was happening in the group around her. I still did not allow her to talk in the groups and when we tried to work on her, her stuff melted like ice. Nothing to grasp. Nothing to see. All would trickle away, evaporate in the heat.

About that time, I had a call from the Institut in Florida. Some problem with tax lawyers and charitable status. So – I should not tell you this, should I? I must trust you and I tell you to make the point that now I see how carefully I should have watched her. Now I understand the magnitude of my failure to observe.

Enough. I can say no more. I am a professional concern. In America you may phone toll-free to get the rates. All therapy is extra on top of the basic residence and shared groups. Two colonics thrown in. Dolphin involvement (seasonal restrictions) is $1000 per day. Invoices must be settled on departure.

The past, the past I tell you, has a compulsion, a grip, which the present cannot even begin to exert. For Maria, this crossroads of so many people's personal histories, this place in which they attempted to confront the agonies of their pasts, this was her present. It was mine too, but into my own history I was too securely locked. What place for Maria's desires? You may watch and you will see.

In the sleepy, will-destroying heat of the Mediterranean mid-afternoon, the moral imperatives of men thinking in chill garrets in the winters of German university towns are as nothing, straws before a forest fire. I would like to pour a ton of frozen peas upon these two women, to show how cold it is for some of us. If God believes that the IRS should for to close the Florida Institut then so be it. They know nothing.

I am a fat little man – my mother Italian, my father German – also some baldness of the head, stumbling blindly on the rocks, thinking I am shipwrecked while only a few metres from my own front door.

It is not appropriate to laugh. Enough, now. I should have foreseen. But my radar was all shot from importation of family romance to my island, my sanctuary.

Maybe, as the textbooks say, the falsehoods which the subject chooses to share are more fundamental than the facts. You are thinking that making movies is simpler than this – maybe you are not so wrong. Turn away from your creation, even for a moment, and the fallen Prince will start to plot disquiet.

But it is a disgusting thing to lose the grip in this way. Please hit me for this. Beat me with a stick about the face and head.

Do it. Hurt me. Thank you. So.

The Institut, let me remind you, is on the headland of a wide bay. Most of the buildings are on the sheltered side of a ridge looking back over the beach which rims the back of the bay. Behind the beach three valleys converge and above them, on the spine of rock which bifurcates the island, two monasteries are perched precariously like the nests of eagles.

A few of my rooms face out to the opening sea, towards two islands in the distance, both maybe ten kilometres away. The neighbour islands in the morning you can clearly see but in the afternoon, the sun now behind them, they are shrouded in a swath of heat. They start to look like shadows or spectres, my platonic Mamma and Pappi reclining on the silvered waves (I wrote slivered just now, instead of silvered – what do you think?).

From my control tower where I have the video console, the telescopes, also the cameras, I can look to the sea, also to the valley and the house of Maria. I have a command position.

OK, so I like to know what is happening around my island. Knowledge, after all, is power. Information – I must have full information. I watch with field glasses (Zeiss), also zoom camera, like a sports photographer. I watch the girls and boys on the beach naked. I watch the houses in the valley, the people on their private terraces. There is nothing

I do not see. A pretty good watch I keep. They think I sleep, but I watch.

First observe, second interpret, third employ your newly interpreted information to advantage. My friend, Michel Foucault (now gone the way of all perverted flesh), this he understood, that all power is a form of oppression. What he was too shallow to admit was that this is what all of us wish. So, seize this power, throw the lightning down from the mount. Be a prince over the world.

I must keep a careful watch over the house of Maria, preset the zoom camera to make a series of time-phase photographs. Thus, even when I am not watching, I am watching. This is my completeness. You must be thorough.

After three weeks, Laura began to show herself. She was becoming thin, the skin golden, hair somehow renewed by sunlight, her movements made with grace, the aspect infused with a strong attraction. No more bottom-wobble.

I allowed her to take off the Silence-in-Group T-shirt and waited to see what would happen. I wanted to shake from her body the powerful toxic trinkets that I could sense there. Her resistance was strong and I decided perhaps some words out of her mouth I must let fall to commence the process.

Mid-group – the heiress junkie, Brigitte, she was telling the others how her father would beat her with the rolling pin from the kitchen drawer. Brigitte's sister would watch, too frightened or too interested to interfere.

In the group many of the faces had the usual expression when such stories are being shared – selfless concern and sympathy on the surface, and from below curiosity and dark empathy seeping through. It was because of this, Brigitte told us, that she took drugs. To myself I was thinking, some analyst told her this and now she offers it to us, a token; a foil. She was complying with rather than trusting the process.

Laura was the first to react.

'I don't believe you,' she said.

Brigitte started to weep.

Didier, the French diplomat, spoke up for once:

'Brigitte speaks the truth of her feelings.' Strange how a diplomat should always choose the wrong moment.

'You keep out of this,' Laura said. 'Stay in the closet, where you belong.'

'I must ask you to speak about yourself,' Maria said. 'You are not here to judge the others.'

'But it's all right for them to judge me?'

'No one is judging you,' I said.

'Bollocks,' Laura said. 'You've kept me in the corner like a naughty schoolgirl so you can formulate clichés about my state of mind. And now, when you permit me to speak, the truth of my instinct – that Brigitte is concocting a tale to win sympathy – is deemed invalid. I know what it's like to watch your father doing things to your sister. I know what it's like and she's lying.'

Laura was shaking. Some current from her was energising the group. I myself could feel a judder in my bones. Bruce/Daisy struggled to his feet like a drunk man. 'I'm not comfortable with this.'

'Not as uncomfortable as you will be.'

The tension was a siren rising up the scale. A chorus of sirens breaking into minor chords. Next to Laura, the Texan bulimic, Louette, was pale with fear. 'I want out of this,' she said.

Laura turned on her – 'I've listened to you moping for three weeks, nursing your sickly inner child, changing its wet nappies, holding it to your scrawny tit. Now you can listen to me for a while.'

'This is connecting me with a lot of stuff,' Bruce/Daisy said. 'I feel very threatened by Laura's verbal abuse.'

'You earn three feeling points, Bruciedaze,' Laura said. 'What the fuck do you know about abuse, you little fag.'

There were some moments of absolute, trilling silence.

'What do you know about abuse, Laura?' Maria asked.

'I know', Laura said, 'that you have to ask for it. To want it. Then you get what's coming to you.'

General consternation in the group. This statement did not fit with their received ideas about such things. I wanted to know what she would say next. I was not prepared.

'And as for these inner children you all bang on about,' Laura said, 'make no mistake – they are gone. Dead. Vanished. Puff! Buried. You can't reclaim them.'

Laura stood and paced around the outside of the circle. 'Unless—' She stood still.

'Unless what?' Maria asked.

'Don't think you can trust Herr Institut Direktor any more than the parents who expelled you from the womb, flung you from their bosoms, shoved you unprepared into a predatory waiting world. Until—'

'Until?'

'I have an announcement to make.' Laura walked more quickly around the circle, wheeling around us like a bird. 'I want this announcement recorded. In point of fact, I am confident that it is being recorded. Aren't I, Herr Direktor?'

'We are listening,' I said. 'We hear you.'

'You hear everything, don't you?' She stopped circling and addressed the group. 'If you've ever had that feeling that you're being watched and thought, no, no, stop being paranoid, think again. Our podgy healer watches us all day long. You can't pick your nose or take a shit without him recording it, replaying it, analysing it. And you believe he does it for your well-being?'

Why should I report this to you? You must understand, dear future client, just how damaged the soul can become; just how much one such as Laura needs my place of healing. Even when it seemed to her a place of torture and deception. Especially then.

'You must understand – all of you. Let it be known and let the knowledge sink into you like a wellington boot in a bog: there is no redemption.' She was almost shouting now. 'Whatever the fuck they tell you – another week will help, try a colonic, swim with the dolphins, buy a rebirthing course, go to Florida for the EST weekend. Nothing works. I've tried it. None of it works.

'But you, Franz Marelli-Kreitznacht, Herr Mountebank Institut-Direktor and holiday camp extortionist. You, you, you—'

Screaming—

That was my missed moment.

You might say that Laura was more with the dead, beyond the ferry of Charon, than with us, the living.

Yes, I should have confronted, I should have told. But I confess it to you – I was afraid. Afraid to push her too hard. Afraid of how she would react. This fear I should have overcome and followed my instinct to flush her out once and for all time.

—but screaming in the deep robustness of a male baritone. The voice of a man from the throat of this now pretty, pretty crazy woman.

I did not want to be in the same room.

After, when I played back the tape of the group, it was still there. The gravel-voice of a middle-aged man – full and booming.

She glared at me:

'He peddles the promise of redemption. We pay and pay and pay. We shrink while he bloats, shrivel into battered children and abused pubescents, dysfunctionals and neurotics, aphasics and polypaths while he weaves it all together at a hundred per cent mark-up. And the snake coiling in his heart chokes him and feeds on his blood. We are what we are. But him? Look at him. Look at his eyes. He is the darkness made flesh.'

*　　*　　*

Michaelis did not prepare me for this. Were his notes incomplete? Can it be that he edited them? Did he fail to understand? Was he scared?

Laura rushed from the group room, slamming the door.

Bruce/Daisy was whimpering, Diplomat Didier comforted him with the arm around the shoulder, his hand hovering over Daisy's new breast. Louette slid across the floor, away from the place where Laura had sat, as from a place of infection.

Maria unmesmerised faster then me. She followed Laura out of the room.

At first, I wanted to speak a prayer, but no prayer could I remember. Some phrases gathered in me, but when my mouth opened I could no words say. All I could do was go to each of them in turn and offer my arms in embrace.

Louette was the first I approached. As I came close a look of terror crossed her face. She shrank from me. When I touched her arm she jumped away as from a sting.

I turned to Didier. He shook his head. Not me. Not me.

Brigitte? Eyes to the floor, avoiding mine.

I worked to find my voice, swallowing against a choking fluff in my throat. After a time in all the stillness I found the opening to whisper.

'You have witnessed a transformation. A powerful metamorphosis. Try not to afraid be. Trust, if you can, the process. It cannot harm you. Only heal. Turn to that in which you believe, whether inside or outside yourself. Look in that place and draw strength.'

In the presence of evil, under the shadow, my words were no better than a thumb in the dyke. I watched as my clients rose, one by one, and left the room.

None would look at me.

I remained in the middle of the circle, surrounded by the cushions on which the impressions of my clients were moulded still. It was the middle of the day. The room was dim, the shutters closed. I held the atmosphere of the group, struggling to contain it and understand it before it dispersed. I was husked, scooped out. Shocked. A cold current drew on my heart, pulling me down.

Sometimes the road is hard. To act as the vessel, to contain the poison which spills from the chalice of another – not poison – I was thinking, serum? Semen? I could not find the word.

Venom. Yes, the venom which Laura had spilled. I had tried to contain it, to spare the others and yet not to be poisoned myself.

But they saw the venom in me (in her it had been too deeply hidden) which from her mouth she had spat. They assumed me to be the source of this venom which, my instinct told me, from her father she had inherited.

He suffered this when from the cross He dangled, weighed by the sins of all.

I climbed the circling stairs to my tower and switched the monitor to the camera in Laura's room.

Empty.

The dining room. My patients, eating, whispering. I could not hear what they said.

The whitewashed stairs to the jetty. Nobody.

I went to the telescope and scanned the hillside, the bay. Nothing.

In the darkroom, the photographs from the time-phase camera trained on the house of Maria were drying after development. I assessed the pictures, looking there for some clue: Maria shooing the agricultural policeman (a base one who always comes to stare at her breasts); as usual, many photos empty of people, just with the winkled scatter of red which was geranium flower, strands of vine hanging down untrained; one of Maria standing with arms raised – in greeting, signalling? – standing on the wall of the terrace; another of Maria entering the bedroom and – look! – the arm and the shoulder, the hair of another, just showing in the shadow by the doorway. Who?

Somehow, I was thinking, this venom I must discharge. My desire was to eat, then sleep. But I could not act. I sat behind the zoom camera – not looking through the lens but staring, eyes unfocused, across the bay, to the rim of the beach, the valley, the hills beyond, the outcrop of white which was the monastery up on the ridge, on the spine of the island.

Time passed.

I wound back the videotape of the morning group:

'—shoved you unprepared into a predatory waiting world. Until—'

And later:

'I am confident that it is being recorded. Aren't I, Herr Direktor?'

How did she know, *Gott in Himmel*? And then, when her voice changed.

'—Mountebank Institut-Direktor and holiday camp extortionist. You, you, you—'

The voice down to male depth on the word 'mountebank'. I must look this word up in the dictionary, I thought. I knew it was not so good.

I wound and played, wound and played.

Fine-tuned from years of therapeutic process, my instinct spoke to me. This baritone was her father. And my instinct, you will see, was good.

Maybe I understood this later. But I tell you, see? Nothing do I try to conceal. My heart, also my mind and spirit, I open to you, show the full picture. Three hundred and sixty degrees; 100 per cent; 20/20. This is a privilege. Appreciate, please.

Thank you. And send for the brochure. All can benefit from the process. All can learn to trust the process. Except Laura.

Not for her the healing moment, the balm of self-acceptance, the torch of insight, the voice of reason. She spurned my hospital of love.

What do I sell at mine Institut, if not love? Some of them, whatever price they pay for this most priceless commodity, still they cannot receive it at the till. I have learnt to feel compassion for this condition. But Laura – even if this is what she wanted, wanted beyond anything, her wanting had turned it into another thing.

More to distract me from the chaos, from the dread of facing the patients, than from a hope that I would see anything, I looked through the zoom at the house of Maria in the valley.

There they were: the woman of my right hand and the incubus, walking together up the path from the olive grove to the terrace of Maria's house. Both with wet hair. Swimming? Together?

I undressed.

It was so hot.

Yes, even with the air-conditioning, because to use the zoom I must the shutter open have, also the window, and so, and so—

Why must you question? Even now you have no faith? Quiet, please. Silence. My clothes off I took for I was too hot.

Enough said.

In the canvas direktor's chair I sat, Franz Marelli-Kreitznacht on the back printed. Soon the canvas was damp from my perspiring. I crouched forward to set my eye against the soft rubber of the eyepiece. Thirty-six exposures I had.

Ready to roll. Ready for love.

One shot as they reached the terrace, pulling off their clothes. Below the almond tree is a simple shower. Maria first walks off the terrace – out of view for a moment – reappears by the tree. Water falls. Under the water, the sprinkle under the light, under the flutter of almond-leaf shadow on her skin. Shots two, three, four. Also the glister and sparkle of water falling through light on to her hazel skin. Five, six. The fine contour of her rib-cage as she raised her arms to rub water into her hair, to wash out the salt. The concave below the rib-cage – seven, eight – where the stomach is so perfect, the curve of the breast above. The cold water – nine – on the nipple made it for to point. Click, buzz-whirr (auto-wind, of course, I have). Ten, eleven, twelve.

My zoom is a fat truncheon. I am a policeman of this Maria. She falls under the water. For this I fall. I must punish. Thirteen.

I am not ashamed to say it. I was hardening. The object of beauty, of desire. Before this, in accordance with principles of nature, omphalos must in worship rise. Fourteen. He was half risen now, swinging below the zoom, up and down to twitch. One hand upon the adoration I stroked, the other fingered the shutter release.

All this behaviour was from the venom of Laura.

To me she did. I am reconciled. The struggle she bettered. Also over Maria. Not Laura maybe, but the spectre of her father, incubus of the patriarch, foul bequest, unseemly trust-fund of his unnatural acts. It is the truth I speak.

Fifteen was Laura from behind the wall coming. Stood beside Maria. Did Maria know she was there?

The golden one, the thin one now, transformed from blubber, next to Maria, the hazel and the golden. Possible sisters.

Maria wet in the shower. Laura dry beside her. Click buzz-whirr. Sixteen. Twitch.

They speak. What?

Laura poured liquid from a bottle, on to her hands. Maria bent her head, then down on her knees before Laura. Seventeen.

Shampoo.

Laura with the hands a white froth made in the dark hair of Maria. So hot in my tower. Click, eighteen, buzz-whirr. No twitch can this omphalos make – too hard.

Soon I must the venom for to spill. The cream of shampoo ran in flows of white lava over the breasts of Maria, over the hair of her pubis, down her strong thigh. Nineteen to twenty-two: hands of Laura in Maria's hair.

Now the water washing away the bubbles. The hands sweeping the froth down the back of Maria, touching every which where.

They change around – click, buzz-whirr, twenty-three.

The canvas so damp below my buttocks. The rubber of the eyepiece against the socket of my eye. A little squelchy sound it makes, a suction as I move back from the camera. Laura under the water, on her skin now the light drops, the almond-leaf shadows on her skin shaking. Twenty-four. Myself also shaking.

A gust of wind. My shutter swung loose from its clasp, slammed against the frame, just missing the protrusion of the zoom. Wind also in the valley shook the leaf shadow in a mad dance over the women. The water swept sideways. Light water shadow pouring, falling, swirling in a riot, twenty-five.

Laura was on her knees, Maria with the shampoo. Sweet agony it was to watch my brave strong girl ensnared. Laura on her broomstick, crash landing in my paradise.

Twenty-six, Maria brushes the shampoo from Laura's face, works the froth into her hair. Twenty-seven, Laura's arms around the waist of Maria coil. The knees of Maria buckle and down she slides into embrace of Laura. The glitter of water. Twenty-eight. The pulse of light. Twenty-nine.

Meeting of the skins, hazel and golden, white froth upon the flesh. Thirty.

Venom from my broomstick pours, seeds upon the barren ground. Click buzz-whirr, thirty-one, two, three, four, five and I am done. Thirty-six.

Not my seed, I must tell you. And the progeny? Not mine, not mine.

To the terrace where they dry each other. Click. No film.

Laura peels an orange. Places the segments in the mouth of Maria. Into the bedroom, Maria leading, pulling Laura by the hand.

She looked my way. I cannot know this, yet I know that to the tower she looked. And just as into the bedroom she disappeared, where I could not see, at me she winked. Click. Nothing. I cannot prove.

Already it was too late.

Laura Blade

A hotel on an island.

So much Daddy's sort of thing being as it is redolent of his youth. Isolated within a small community, an isolated community.

The guests a collection of Euroflotsam and United Jetsam.

I am a dried-up sack of sexlessness despite the sun on my skin, the wind in my hair and the sea-salt drying on my lips. But even the taste of the sea will not dispel the chemical taint from my tongue; Haldol, Largactil – my pharmacological bodyguards.

I am out and away and underwater as much as I can be, down with the fish – the Mummy fish and the Billy fish.

I have asked them to call me Arlene.

They take no notice.

None at all.

I'm much more of an Arlene than a Laura.

You can imagine going for an Arlene, can't you?

She's your sort of girl in her cowboy boots and her long-tasselled jacket. Don't you like the sound of that?

Thin as a rake with round high-slung breasts and a narrow face, but look more closely and Arlene's features are pinched and mean. The cheeks of a rodent. Yes, but isn't Arlene the one with her rented mind and her overconditioned hair and her garnished clothes and her frontierswoman boots?

She was something in modern dance until the back injury, and when she wanted to have babies she couldn't, could she?

Poor Arlene.

Poor little Arlene.

Daddy would have fancied an Arlene. Wouldn't he just? Just like he fancied me.

When my heart surges these days, Daddy, Vivian and Billy behind me, my wake revealing the direction in which my bows must point, I surge forward into a new sea where the colours are muddled, waves a smoky ochre frothed by pink surf, the sky darkest green, a racing sky.

On a day when my heart crawls with light, in an hour when certainty robes me like a queen – one beringed hand holding the folds of the heavy shroud across my breast – in that same hour my skin tightens across my cheeks and words fall from my lips like garbage from a split bin-liner. I am stranded on the pavement, a plastic yoghurt pot plastered in carrot peelings, peppered by coffee grounds, awaiting collection.

When I search for love in my heart I find it hidden under a stone in darkness. A trail of gunpowder leads there. Couldn't you have used a piece of string, Daddy? Or crumbs? Manna? Coins? Of all the footprints around the stone yours predominate, familiar outsized missed.

*   *   *

Have I been waiting for him to die all this time? I used to say to my sister Lizzie that he might as well be dead already for all the difference it made or makes or will make. To which she would say, it has nothing to do with him, what he might do or has done. And I continue – nor am I ashamed of it – to allow her to be haunted by him because then I don't have to be.

I say to her no no no no you're your own person, go beyond your parents, realise yourself (sit with yourself, ooh la la, in your own space and get in touch with what it is really like to own your own stuff, be really you). As I say all this I am secretly cradling Daddy's head on my lap while Lizzie beats her head against a daddy who doesn't notice, a daddy who isn't really there at all.

'How thin you are, Arlene. Any thinner and your bones would snap.'

'But I did it all for you, Daddy.'

He has sent me here for a rest.

Rest easy, little girl. To a place where I can take the sun and reacquaint myself with – what? Me? (Laura, Michaelis would say, when are you going to address the issues you have around self-esteem? What do they mean, for God's sake, by the use of 'around' in that context? I detest euphemism, particularly in a preposition.)

Daddy's predilection for the Mediterranean solitude of his youth, for islands; all before every outcrop of rock was crowned with a hotel or flattened for an airstrip.

Out of his solitude Daddy became a maker of things, a maker of himself, a monster hatched from the coupling of bored testosterone and the golden eggs of literature.

There was his mother, of course, the fragrant Isabella. I remember her, before she became a crone, before her fingers became gnarled, her face a web of age, mouth slack, limbs frail. Imagine what a young boy must have thought of her. How much in those long island winters he would have wanted a woman like his mother, yet not his mother, to experiment upon, to fondle.

The hotel in which I languish is built on a series of steps up a hillside and looks out upon a wide bay. We are in Greece – the warm south – with wind all day and much of the night. The rooms are really little bungalows with their own terraces enclosed by screens of bamboo clattering and creaking in the wind. In my little hut I have a shower with a white-tiled floor and where the tiles are cracked I can see the remains of other people's grime: dead skin, body hair, secretions.

In the adjacent hut there is a woman who cries in the evening. I've heard her three nights in a row. Ten minutes before supper, as if she is mourning the meal in advance. A vegetarian?

The sun will have just gone behind the hill and we will all be in our rooms readying ourselves for dinner. Under the wind I hear another voice, not of the wind, but like it. Gusty, determined, relentless. In a lull I hear crying. I am afraid. I want to go to her to comfort her, or to laugh at her absurd sorrow, to say, have you no gratitude? Can't you see how lucky you are to be in this marvellous hotel with the sea and the wind and the companionable guests?

Just the other side of the bamboo, close enough to touch. But I don't reach out. I sit and listen to her sob and I think to myself: it serves you right. Brigitte. French. An heiress to boot. Pathetic. Drug addicts get what's coming to them. I mean, who do they think they are to suppose that they can sit around on the nod all day and still command our sympathy? I ask you.

At dinner she is immaculate. No puffiness about the eyes, make-up precise. She must have a tape-recording of someone weeping. Or is it the sound she makes when she's being fucked? But by whom? Can I meet him?

I contrive to sit next to her. She is pretty, or could be.

But something has turned her skin to crumpled paper, twisted her body so that she is always wrapping her arms around herself, crossing and uncrossing her legs. Never comfortable.

She is friends with Maria.

I want to be friends with Maria.

The hotel food is passable. No alcohol is served. Guests are encouraged to mix at large tables. Like the clubs that Daddy's friends have in London. The manager Franz and his assistant Maria join us for dinner, as if we were at sea. Let Franz's be the captain's table: a delicate dance, a prelude to each dinner, as we manoeuvre to avoid sitting next to him. Like all evangelists, he lacks conversation.

There are twenty of us. Perhaps more. A hotel for single people. A hotel dedicated to tranquillity, peace and quiet. A hotel in which a French heiress weeps every evening before dinner.

'My father was raised on an island like this one. Peasants, you know, and the beginnings of a tourist trade.' I was attempting conversation. Nothing wrong with that.

Brigitte did not reply. I have heard her speaking perfectly good English so she cannot claim not to understand. Strange the way people take against me right from the start. As if forewarned that I am a bad lot.

Brigitte stared at her food – a grilled fish and a stuffed tomato. Was the prospect of eating a source of embarrassment to her? From across the table Maria, the manager's assistant, rescued me:

'Which island?'

I told her about the Italian islanders commanded by their priest to go to Australia to make money. My daddy was a member of the following generation and returned as a thirteen-year-old to an island that had been almost deserted for twenty-five years. The story gushed out of me and I muddled some of it up. But if Maria did not understand, she concealed her incomprehension behind a smile. At your service.

'Daddy turned from jackaroo into ragazzo over the course of a summer. After he died his will told us he wanted to be buried on the island but my mother refused. She denied him even that. Can you believe it?'

Maria was encouraging me by her look to say more. Brigitte lit a cigarette. Maria told her she could not smoke between courses.

'Your father—'

'Please, there is no reason why you should have known,' I said. 'I am quite reconciled. I have grieved.'

Brigitte started to cry. Maria came around the table and held her. I too put a hand on her shoulder – I could not touch more of her than that. Because she smelt. Something wrong with her liver or her glands. She smelt of boiled cabbage. Maria clasped her all the same and led her away from the table.

I will have to be more demonstrative to claim attention around here. Rather than upsetting Brigitte I had done her a service, delivering her into Maria's arms, arms that might have encircled my blobby bulk and guided me to my room. Next time.

I have pills. To make me sleep. I wait each night until the choir between my ears is singing so loudly that it beats out the wind. Then I submit. Twenty minutes later I drown.

I awake choking as if my lungs have filled with bile. I cough for some minutes and then I light a cigarette.

For these first days they are leaving me to myself. They hate me. All of them.

Maria too. And who can blame them? I am the last to point the finger. But when I do it will be loaded, with the safety off.

The guests gather each morning in the public rooms of the hotel, muttering over breakfast and newspapers.

They shoo me away. Go snorkelling, they say. Enjoy the sunshine.

In other words, fuck off. And then they follow me. They watch.

It's spangly. The rocks are friendly under the water, the voices of the waves silenced. What's behind me? Just blue deepening to murky grey, the descent towards the big emptiness where the fat fish, the ocean's bully boys, wallow in the chill. There's nothing to get hysterical about. We all need to rest from time to time, deserve a break from the humming factory of self. But, my, has the factory been busy. We've been working time and a half.

Maybe they are right that I need some sort of geographical equivalent for my state. I become preoccupied by the colours, by the architecture of this underworld. I drop down below the surface to follow a shoal of rainbow-ribbed fish and forget how cold I am. Even blubbery me. I look above the surface, the sound of the waves returning, and see that I have drifted some distance from my entry point, from my towel on the rocks. That should tell me something, shouldn't it? That should jolly well stand for something.

If Lizzie were here she'd be able to tell me.

I have some photographs with me. Of the family, such as it is. Such as it was. Rather suburban, isn't it, lugging the family snaps around. I'll be knitting next and collecting for the local borstal open-day sandwich fund.

One photograph – I have stuck it up on the wall of my hut in the whitewashed hotel compound – shows the drawing room of our house in the country before the break-up. Daddy looks so young. He's on the window-seat gazing down at either me or Lizzie.

I can't tell which. We were no more than eighteen months old at the time the photograph was taken. And then there is the dog. A dog I loved. I cannot for the life of me – lie awake at night reeling off doggie names as I might – recall her name. My/Lizzie's hand is on

Daddy's leg. We are twisting around to look at something beyond the photographer. The dog stands beside me/Lizzie, a black labrador wearing a look of dignified, long-suffering sorrow in contrast to the strained to-order smiles of the humans.

I/Lizzie sit on a patterned rug of browns and burnt reds, cream, orange – Iberian Arab in design and tone. At the bottom of the picture there is a pair of – holes? Mirrors? Ponds? Flames? And between the two small semi-circular silver pools, a beast's horn? A dead tree? An embryonic hand? The rug is about to burst into flame.

I have told myself, putting on my most sensible and reassuring voice, that the image is a processing aberration, a chemical splash. But I don't buy it.

I cannot decide whether it is Lizzie or me sitting on that rug.

What are they speaking of while I am away? Are they cloistered in silence? Have I stumbled across some sect in summer retreat? What casualties are these waiting for shriving?

I am better off on my own. I have inherited Daddy's island-fostered inclination for solitude. In him it bred a boorish melancholy, a bleakness he called determination.

And with only his mother Isabella to turn to, how far did he turn? Alone with her in a big empty hotel all winter. They must have discovered some comforts in one another's arms. Sweating and heaving in the high old bed. A rosary hung from the bedpost, rattled on the wood to the beat of their drum.

I have read it in his notebooks – faded ring-bound exercise books in the bottom drawer of his desk. Jejune espials, watching her undress, the glow of her skin by candlelight, his overflowing love, their tender exuberances; a cornucopia of euphemisms.

Flesh stung to submission, beaten like copper, chipped like stone, boiled and braised like cabbage. Goosebump flesh like – well – like the flesh of a goose. The prodigal daughter of the prodigal son; we spend and spend.

At supper the next evening, after the keening vespers in the next-door hut, I found a place at table next to Maria.

With minimal self-prompting I wept into my salad. I hate to be bettered.

I continued to shovel food into my mouth, swallowing olive stones. Maria held my free hand. My throat was tight from crying. I swallowed against the muscular constriction. More like taking a shit than eating.

Pliant, scorched by the sun, trembling.

She forced me to it.

So often the Greek women are short and dark, verging on the swarthiness of their male counterparts. Certainly plain and lumpy, the aesthetic favours having been shared unequally between the Hellenic genders.

But Maria was from Macedonia. Quite unconnected to the peasant stock of the islands. Green eyes.

Bump-starting sorrow is fine as long as you can turn off the engine when you choose. But I couldn't stop. Maria led me from the dining room. As we passed Brigitte, she gave me a mean little glance. What is this place? Heartbreak Hotel?

Maria pushed open the door and we entered my stuffy room. She eased me on to the bed and opened the shutters. A rush of cooler air on my cheek. Cicadas sawed away at the trees on the terrace above.

When I had her full attention, I told her about Joy Fairweather:

'In England, it is considered a mark of affluence and social status to be able to send your children away, at the earliest possible opportunity, to live in a barracks. The standards of food and accommodation are in inverse proportion to the fees. Each school of five or six hundred is divided up into houses of fifty or sixty. In my house we had five dormitories. Ten girls to a dormitory. You got along with those ten girls or you were doomed. Sent to Coventry – sorry – outcast.

'My sister Lizzie – she'll be here soon, she's joining me; I wish she would just hurry up and get here – anyway, Lizzie was teased for her large breasts – bazonkas, boobies, wonderbra. Thirteen-year-olds can be relentless. I was her protectress. At first, I deflected attention from her by playing the clown, then the storyteller. I made a fool of myself and they would forget about Lizzie as they laughed at me. Flies feeding on the nearest carcass.'

'Did you not tell one of the teachers what was happening?'

'There was a code, like honour among thieves. If you told on another girl it would only make things worse. The worst of them was Joy Fairweather. She had the bed in between mine and Lizzie's. She would not let up. Every night after lights-out she would whisper taunts – who's your boyfriend? Did you suffocate him? Why does everyone hate you? Why are you such a tart? Camilla says your father made his money out of smuggling. You're a wop, aren't you?'

'—?—'

'A foreigner. On and on, question after rhetorical question, taunt after taunt, night after night, for months. Joy was tall and blonde, pretty in the way that horses are pretty. She had a talent for intimidation and she was archetypal of the English middle classes, the personification of norms from which Lizzie and I deviated unacceptably. We learnt to be ashamed of being different. Very important to correspond to the standard. The other girls deferred to Joy. Fearing her, they echoed her attacks on Lizzie, knowing their collaboration would spare them from her attacks. Brigitte is another Joy Fairweather. You learn to spot the type.'

'I think you are wrong about Brigitte. She is more a Lizzie

than a Joy,' Maria said. 'Remember, this is not like school. You are safe here.'

I'd like a kiss for every time that's been said to me.

'I'm an abductress, you know. A thief and a cheat and a destroyer of people's lives.' I gave it to her straight.

'That must make you feel very important and powerful.'

'I don't expect you to believe me,' I said. 'People don't believe me.'

Maria sat on the low stool by the window. I lay on the bed.

'I don't remember how, but it became clear that Joy liked me. Physically, I mean. She wasn't gay, but she was sexual and there were only girls to be sexual with. I wasn't so fat then. Do you hate me being this fat? Don't answer.

'One day, in the changing rooms – this was during a period when Joy was physically bullying Lizzie, inciting the other girls, punching Lizzie on the upper arms where the bruises wouldn't show – I found myself alone with Joy, towelling down after showers. She watched me dressing, an alien heavy-liddedness to her gaze. I couldn't have articulated it at the time but I had a sort of power over her. I let my towel drop, stood naked while I searched for my underwear in the tangle of clothes on the changing-room bench. Her eyes crawled over me. I took my time.'

A glance confirmed that I had Maria's full attention. A gust of wind swung the unlatched shutters against the wall of the hut with a clap.

'Go on,' she said.

I stood up and walked to the window. On the other side of the mosquito gauze the moon had not yet risen. The black murk might have been Berkshire or Manhattan or the end of the world.

'I wanted to control her. We were all so scared of her. It was loveless and mechanical. I learnt how to give her pleasure. For a day or two afterwards she was tender, treated me and Lizzie as part of her circle. We belonged. She gave us cigarettes. Lizzie had some peace.

'Then, just when I thought it had worked, she would call me a tart in front of the other girls and we would be on the outside again. Before long they would be taunting Lizzie about her breasts, then hitting her. I would fuck Joy. And so on. As reliable as the tide.'

'Your parents could have stopped this,' Maria said.

'Lizzie swore me to secrecy,' I said. 'She preferred school.'

'I must go back,' Maria said. 'We can talk more tomorrow.'

'Won't you come for a swim with me?'

'I'm on duty.'

'Am I not part of your duty?'

'I am here for you, Laura,' she said. 'You don't have to win me.'

The nerve of it. How dare she? Who does she think she is? A squat little peasant with a few weeks' hotel management training in Hounslow or whatever the Greek equivalent is.

'Please don't go.'

'You can call a group if you want to.'

'Don't be absurd.'

She walked clean out of the room. So much for getting your needs met.

I have certainly made a friend of Maria. Oh yes. She has encouraged the hotel manager to admit me to the gatherings they convene each morning. I'm not sure if I really came here to participate in community activities. What did I expect: deck coits? Bridge fours? A sewing circle?

It turned out to be more like church. Church in the round. Ghastly hugging. The guests in a circle, cushions on the tiled floor. Franz and Maria part of the circle. A space for me beside Louette, the spindly one who must be anorexic or something. Can you imagine anyone wanting to do that? Stuffing themselves with food and then puking up? Bulimia. That's what they call it. Disgusting. Hateful.

You wouldn't catch me doing that. Not on your nelly. The stomach acids that break down food during digestion will, in those who vomit on a regular basis, rot the lining of the oesophagus. The subject will suffer the constant discomfort of heartburn.

13

I told you it was a hotel because—

Well, because it's like a hotel.

Except more expensive.

Let me read to you from the brochure:

At the Cycladic Institut the staff have created a tranquil environment in which the guests can relax and free themselves from the strains of busy existences.

And later:

There are moments in every person's life when a reassessment can be invaluable. At the Institut, a broad range of healing strategies are available, administered by experts in timeless seclusion with absolute confidentiality.

A place, you see, in which the well get better. And I have never been better. Never felt so absolutely in command of myself. Of course I worry about Daddy (even though he's dead) and Lizzie. But in the end I must let them go, mustn't I? Let them find their own way. I feel compassion for others. Things can get so dreadfully on top of one. It can happen to just about anyone.

One shouldn't be stigmatised for getting into a bit of muddle, should she?

One has to live with the consequences of one's behaviour. For ever.

This should be perfectly simple, like equations, but it isn't. Not for one. One regrets nothing.

That's how Mummy talks.

The wind has got itself into a bother, clattering the bamboo outside my hut. I was at the border of sleep a moment ago. It is often the way. Just as I am getting my passport ready I begin to remember things, unhappy things. Vivian clocking me; a bald person like an androgynous embryo gazing at me from the mirror; Vivian holding yellow flowers at the hospital and me becoming labile so the butch nurse had to inject me with lead-lining.

Do these events belong to me? They don't feel like mine. Can one feel possessive about memories? Are they owned as one (there she is again) owns scarves and handbags and guilt? He knows that memory is my last sanctuary and he's in there, despoiling and ransacking, looting and polluting.

Now I'm going to take one's pill and glide away.

Wouldn't you?

Daddy was the youngest of six – Catholics. He returned from the Antipodes to a volcanic island populated by doomy half-wits. A manchild, surfing the testosterone flood, he indulged in three moons of frenzied Don Juanism. Artificially demi-orphaned – his father wedded to a soft-drinks franchise in New South Wales, refusing a return to Italy – he was thirsty for a spectrum of sensations about which he had read in Flaubert and Rilke but not yet experienced (nor had he yet met anyone who had thus experienced). His girls always less beautiful and enigmatic than Nick Carraway's Daisy. His sense of existential confusion a mere flutter in the stomach compared with the sufferings of K.

Goaded by a gadfly of lack, he burned for sentiments that perhaps never occurred outside the golden decades of the European novel. Poor Daddy. He believed those books enshrined the secret of his success: Dorothea Brooke in britches.

It's all there in his notebooks. How he would watch his mother undress when he was thirteen. His obsession with her breasts which were, by his account, perfectly formed and made him ooze with desire.

When they arrived on the Italian island they were rowed in from the steamer to the black shore, there being no jetty at which the big boat could dock. The oarsman mistook them for a Roman woman and her tupping boy.

Isabella was togged to the nines, larking really, her sartorial grandness equally out of keeping with the sheep farm from which she had come and the peasant island on which she was landing. The intervening cosmopolitanism of shipboard and Rome had shown her all sorts of sophistications which she had been able to note, absorb and then display, in her clothes, her walk, her look.

Daddy was six shaves into manhood.

On their first night on the island they slept in a run-down taverna, sharing a matrimonial bed, their identities not yet declared. They were pretending, yes, pretending, to be lovers.

Choice, very choice.

I have read his notebooks. All of them, from cover to cover. Who did he think he was, writing in the third person? Marcel? Laurie Lee? Julius Caesar?

Her nightgown was loose and fell away from the throat as she bent down to climb on to the bed. Candlelight billowed into the gap to reveal her nipples hard from the chill. His belly surged. There would be no sleep for him that night.

Son or lover, David Herbert Lawrence, good night.

He cupped her breasts in his hands and felt their exquisite weight. He regressed to her nipples, licking her to drowsy joy.

Turned his mother into a literary device, choirs of angels singing her to sleep.

But did he fuck her? That's what I want to know.

The Direktor of the Institut is a certain Franz Marelli-Kreitznacht. A polymorph, a polypath, a perv. His spasmic urges are held in check, but only just. A nudge or two and my guess is he'd flower into overwhelm.

So, why do I like him?

Most mornings I pop into the kitchen to top up. I cannot survive on what they allow me, so I have befriended the kitchen staff. I add salt to the Greek bread. I have been rather naughty about the bread. Each of us is more than the sum of her symptoms.

Worst of all is the hugging. Why do I let them do it? Why couldn't I just report on my bowel movements like the nervously broken-down Armenian chap? I could manage that all right.

The couple from Boston – binge drinkers who have concealed their alcoholism from the world and each other for twenty years – are being taught to give each other shiatsu massage (and by the by I have seen both of them at the vodka down by the jetty, one at night, the other during siesta). I could do that too.

But the hugs. My armpits prickle. I start to sweat ten minutes before the group, puffing away at a cigarette on the terrace under the palm tree. By the time the cushions are arranged, the blinds adjusted so the hard morning light is filtered, I am on the point of choking. Drenched in sweat. The snake in my gut shifts and slithers about.

Maria first. She is gentle and thin and soft. I pretend that she is Lizzie, which gets me through. I stand. She stands. We walk to the middle of the room. She encircles me in her arms, holds me like a child. I shrink within her embrace. Today I am able to lift my arms from my sides and place them on her shoulders. By the time she releases me, my lower lip is wobbling. I want to fly away. Next Didier. A French diplomat with halitosis. The Boston wife. Almost as fat as I have sometimes been: an awkward and perfunctory clasp with a mutual ejecting thrust to conclude. Louette, anorexic bundle of sticks who has to be handled carefully. Then Dario, a boy with pink swollen hands like inflated washing-up gloves. He presses a half-erection against my stomach. And another fifteen of them until we reach Franz. Me in the middle of the circle, sobbing and snivelling and fisting tissues. The most humiliating thing since school. And it gets worse.

Franz approaches. He puts his hands on my elbows, holds me at arm's length and looks at me for an age before he draws me to him.

Every Friday night when we got to the country – that look of loving inspection, then the clasp.

Franz is a short man. Not at all like Daddy physically. Short and plump, blond hair thinning, a moustache you could not wear in England without being classified a screamer. Eyes blue and small. The sun still burns his face unevenly despite his many years as Cycladic hotelier, guru and health insurance wizard.

But it is a kind face. Despite his posturing insecurity, his anality and his aura of deviancy, his hug, when it surrounds me, is a place in which I am happy to stay, curled up, sleepy. As he releases me, I grip him more tightly. He walks me back to my place in the circle. We are an ill-matched couple, struggling through the waltz, hearing different musics.

I am not allowed to talk. Not a word. My best weapon locked in the gun cupboard. For the moment I am an understudy watching the play, mouthing my lines, waiting for a calamity to befall one of the principal actors. My time will come.

The days pass. I swim. And then the nights.

I have started to sleep soundly in the afternoons, without medication. One evening, feeling refreshed from my slumber, I wandered up to the top of the compound to watch the sun drop behind the next hill. There I found Dario of the swollen hands and the foul-breathed diplomat.

After that evening, it became our habit to watch the sunset together. The westernmost terrace is higher than any other point in the institute with the exception of the square tower in which Franz's private apartments are housed. Thus, part of the interest in the sunset ritual is that we can catch glimpses from the high terrace of our leader in his elevated bunker. We all know, but do not mention to one another, that it is more Franz than the sunset that we have gathered to watch.

The tower is imposing. Even when the soft tangerine light of the dropping sun falls upon the white blankness of the tower's west wall, the very scale and blindness of it alarm me. It is surrounded by a pubic tangle of young fig trees.

Vivian hit me in the car. You shouldn't hit women.

You really shouldn't and yet so many of you do. So many of us let you believe that we like it. All right, sometimes we don't mind, but it has to be in context. The hitting shouldn't start before the nice things have happened. Vivian I forgive. It's in his nature, innit? Well, doll, I dun wot I dun, and so on.

If he is teachable it is not by the methods of Her Majesty's rehabilitation to which he is probably now once again exposed. I hope his missus takes him some decent smokes.

There is something ratty or vole-like about Franz. Feral. But his features belie him. At least I think they do. Good face to paint.

I will never paint again. Never.

When I offered to do Daddy's portrait he refused to sit for it. So I used photographs and being unsure which one to work from I alternated between three. When I finished, I asked him round for a drink, the picture in the middle of the room on an easel, awaiting his response.

It was a good portrait – it didn't look like him exactly, but it was of him in a more fundamental sense.

He refused to notice it. Chatted about this and that, interrogating me about my life under the guise of parental interest and concern, containing his policing curiosity inside a cloak of smiling daddiness. The picture sat between us like a chaperone, taking note of our conversation, observing what we said and what we left unsaid. I glanced towards it, hoping to shift his eyes to it. Couldn't be done. It was as if he could not actually see that there was a painting in the middle of the room, let alone a painting of him, by me.

What was he so afraid of seeing? Daddy was successful enough in his declared business – import, export, media ownership – to have had his portrait painted three times by artists other than me. The portraits hang in a row over the mantelpiece in the study of his London house.

Later I sent him a large transparency of the picture but he returned it, the package resealed. Lizzie took it in the end, but she hung it in the corner of her hall where you have to seek it out to look at it. It makes her uncomfortable, she says. She sees in it a Daddy she would rather not see. But she has given him a home. Something he wouldn't do for himself. As Daddy no longer visits her, it is unlikely that he will ever see himself.

I could have had them show it to him before they pushed him, my hired assassins. Forced him to look at himself, to see only himself in his slow, final moments.

Rather late in the day to get his attention, but his attention was never a thing I found easy to claim.

On the top terrace of the Cycladic Institute saluting the

demise of Apollo, smoking cigarettes with Dario and Didier,
I brush the Daddy cobwebs from the corners of my consciousness. Tonight there is a new moon, a modest sliver
over the southern ridges which will subside into the sea
before midnight. It will catch the sun's light after the sun
itself has sneaked from view over the western ridge.

I glance over my shoulder, trying once again to identify
the clicking sound that I have often heard while we gaze the
day away. There is a fat truncheon hanging from the high
window of Franz's tower. A long telescopic lens like those
used by sports photographers. The truncheon dips towards
us then up to the horizon.

I could talk to Dario and Didier. That they could only
partly understand me and seldom responded encouraged
me to talk more.

Lorry talks ten to the dozen. Lorry should learn to listen to
something other than the sound of her own voice. Lorry,
you have so much talk and so little to say.

Thanks, Mum.

If Bet said a tenth of the amount that you do, wouldn't
it be a relief? I'm sure your loquaciousness silences her.

My what?

Talkativeness. You're a chatoholic.

If only you had listened, just a little.

'Towards the end of Billy, a syncopated finale in which we
continued to sleep with one another on an occasional and
perfunctory basis long after I had aborted whatever seed
had been sprouting between us, I gave up on sex. At least
my body did.'

Dario grinned inanely at the bay. Didier studied his
cuticles.

'My womb was dry. None of the regular tactical foreplays
would irrigate me. Cunt's a dustbowl, as my gay friend
Augustus says of his mother. Mean old queen. Nothing

regular has excited me since then and that's – what? Nine months? Jesus. And then Vivian.

'When I was a child I thought that holidays was a place, like Hartlepool or South Croydon. When are we going to Holidays?'

'Porto Ercole,' Dario said. 'Vacations.'

'I was raped in New York City – by a chauffeur who was supposed to convey me to the opening of my show in SoHo, Stopped the one-way-glass limo, hopped in the back and schtumped me. He was wearing ghastly trainers with his ill-fitting uniform. He had trouble with his flies. We were parked by a fire hydrant. The police started knocking on the windows before he could come, saving me the sticky knickers bit. Later I was repatriated. When I was thirteen I had an abortion.'

Dario wanted to know what rape meant and I tried to explain with gestures. Was Didier laughing at Dario's obtuseness or at the body syntax with which I sought to enlighten the balloon-handed Italian?

The days passed. And the nights.

If I had been properly listened to at the right time by the right people none of this would have been necessary. None of the things leading to this necessity would have happened or they would have happened differently and led to different necessities – husband, children, a career, a house, a home, troops of friends, babies and cots and Lanaircell blankets and bottle sterilisers. Comforters and climbing frames and Scrabble sets and driving lessons. School fees insurance and grandparental trust-funds. The bras you wear to breast-feed with zippable flaps for left and right nozzle. Clothes for the children. Tiny shoes.

Family. Who needs it?

Something's up with Franz and Maria. A current flows

between them. High-voltage. They make each other crackle
and hum. It's not a love thing, at least I don't think it is. He
may want her but at the moment it's no cigar. Nor is it a
power struggle. The only way I can find to describe it is
to say that she treats him rather like a father and he her
like a mother. But neither responds: he does not play the
father nor she the mother. A stalemate which in Franz's
demotic we may term a symbiosis of negative introjects.
Such stand-offs require a catalytic infusion from without.
Perhaps I can oblige.

For the moment they are after me to have the colonic
irrigation treatment. I've lost plenty of weight. I don't see
the point. I don't buy the mind-body holistic, bits-of-your-
soul-in-your-toes bollocks. We live in a world where even
our bowel movements must be policed and healed.

Tonight I will submit to the tranquillizers and swear off
supper. And no bread attacks or choc-stops or fizzy-drinks
drinking. What do you suppose the record is for the
number of resolutions made and broken in a twenty-four-
hour span?

I must contact Guinness about that.

14

I must tell you.

I completely lost it with the sewing circle this morning. That's what comes of letting me speak. I don't know what they were all whingeing about.

As for Franz, I am quite sure that he is spying on us all. I'm sure of it. To what end, I don't know. A strange hotel in which the management permits itself the privilege of watching the guests at their toilet, in the privacy of their bedrooms.

Perhaps it's not so unusual. Am I naive?

I refuse, at any rate, to be treated like a sick child in an observation ward watched over by a lecherous middle-European whose cupidity seems bent upon voyeurism and the fast buck in equal measure. Maria, as far as I can make out, shares our status of innocent victims. Does she know that he watches? Does she secretly tolerate it? Does she approve?

So I threw a wobbly in the middle of the sewing circle. There we all were: Dario, Louette, Brigitte, Didier, the Bostonians and the rest, all mewling and moaning and going on.

I spilt the beans about our ever-watchful manager and gave the guests a morale-boosting lecture. Schoolmistressy, reproving, a *tour de force*, working up a good head of steam and broiling them with it, telling them how it is, helping them to see it straight. Protect and serve. Serve and volley. Cannon and fugue.

Then Daddy did something terrible. God knows, and God no doubt abhors whatever power it is that he has.

I spoke in his voice. I was winding up my tirade, little Franz in a lather, when out of my mouth slopped the voice of John Blade, deep, rumbling, raspy, gravelled, booming.

Mortification in the sewing circle. I was as frightened as they looked. I dragged us out of there as fast as I could.

My main concern was to kill myself as quickly as possible. Drowning was the nearest option to hand. I ran down the whitewashed steps to the jetty and flung myself at the water in a swallow dive, wings out wide.

I tried to die but he wouldn't let me. I wanted to breathe water but he forced me to burst through the surface for air, made me live on. My incubus, my darling Dad.

I was under again, trying to breathe water, when a splash beside me announced a torpedo shrouded in a swirl of bubbles. Hands pulled me to the surface. I fought. We went under again. My saviour – if she had but known that drowning might have saved me – was stronger.

'Little girl,' she said to me. 'Don't do this.'

She wanted me to go back to the hotel with her, to change. I didn't dare open my mouth. I shook my head.

She took me by the hand and led me over the rocks to a narrow goat track. We wound up and down and around and about, sometimes inland, other times up on the cliff overlooking the water, between brutal rock formations. They almost broke into tongue. On one rock, a smooth panel covered in what looked like cuneiform writing. Others blown and washed to razor sharpness, masses tumbled halfway down the hill and frozen there, poised to fall further. A petrified bestiary. A giant armadillo with a sword-spine; a tiger twisting its head towards the sea. An iguana, again with the samurai sharpness along the spine.

Holes in the yellow rocks made ears, eyes, mouths. I wanted to give up. Maria pulled me on, sure-footed, steady, silent.

When we were past the stone zoo, the path descended through olive groves, terrace by terrace, past the back of another hotel to the beach. We walked along the shore holding hands, our clothes almost dry now.

Naked men and women stretched out on the sand stared at us as we passed. One man with hair on the top of his shoulders leered at us.

Halfway along the beach I looked back and saw the hotel, a stack of white wedges cut into the hillside halfway between the shore and the headland where the bay opened out to the sea. And rising from the white wedges, the erect tower of the German-Italian hotelier.

We turned inland and struggled through a finer sand which dragged at our ankles and burned our feet. Then over a dusty road and through a wooden gate, across a field where the gnarled and broken roots of vines were paralysed rats, to a broken wall and a terrace where three olive trees made an oasis of shade. Beyond a chump of cactus there was a little house with an almond tree dropping leaf-shadows.

I was vibrant with the beauty of the place. From across the bay, in the institute compound, Maria's house looks like nothing, a blob of white on the hill above the beach. It seemed cruel that everything was allowed to be so beautiful.

Maria sat me in a wicker chair and brought me a glass of water.

I sipped.

She peeled off her skirt and knickers in a single bundle. Then her T-shirt. So brown and thin and perfect. I wanted to tell her how beautiful she was but I could not trust my voice to be mine. She walked down the steps at the end of the terrace and climbed on to a little stone platform under the almond just below where I was sitting. The showerhead had been installed inside the overhang of the branches.

Maria turned the tap and water spilled on her skin, making her darker, lovelier still. Water and shadows shook in the wind, shrouding her in a caul of light and shade. Everything worshipped her.

I pulled off my clothes. I could not speak. As I walked along the terrace to descend the steps something flashed, bright, sharp, distant, in the corner of my eye. I looked out to sea but could not determine the source of the light-splinter.

When I reached the almond-tree shower, Maria's blind hand was reaching along the ledge, fumbling for the shampoo. I took the bottle, poured into my cupped hand and worked lather into her black, black hair. She knelt on the concrete floor of the shower that I could better wash her hair. Then I guided her head back under the stream of water and swept the lather from her head, from her shoulders, wiped it from her back, her breasts.

'Now you,' she said, rising.

I knelt in the shower to be cleansed. She was no longer Maria or Lizzie but someone who was neither of them or both of them. Both neither and both. Because I could not speak I did not have to name her. I understood the curse of naming visited upon Adam and knew the freedom of the unnamed garden.

I hugged her waist as she washed my hair. She slid down within the circle of my arms until we knelt together under the cold water. Having saved me she owned me. I was her chattel.

We dried each other on the terrace.

'I will find you clean clothes,' she said. I nodded and followed her. As I was about to enter the bedroom, I saw the flash again. This time I was able to place its source. I blinked from the dazzle of it, blinked again to clear my vision. The flash came from sunlight reflected off a truncheon protruding from Franz's tower across the bay.

When we were clothed, both in thin loose dresses, Maria

lay me down on the bed and stroked my damp hair. When I woke, she was still stroking my head.

I wanted to talk but at first I was afraid. I could only whisper.

'We were all very young,' I started.

'Lizzie was the first girl who really meant something to him. Billy was seventeen, full of testosterone and tetrahydrocannabinol and he wanted to fuck her partly because he wanted to fuck anyone who wanted to fuck him. There was something else as well, but I didn't have the radar to recognise it, or I was too frightened to let myself see it.

'He was terrified of real involvement, as seventeen-year-old boys are. And yet there was something about Lizzie which compelled him. I don't know.

'You look so like her. The first time I saw you – it was like seeing a ghost. I knew he loved her, and later, too late, he knew it too, but he didn't have words to express it when it counted. They did it once in Daddy's bedroom. Kind of a transgressive breach. She was fucking the full weight of his disapproval as well as Billy.

'My parents were divorced by this time. Man, Billy used to say, are they weird people. Mummy the ice queen, sort of like a fish which has learnt to breathe out of water and mix a decent cocktail but hasn't picked up anything else about what it is to be human. She was in London.

'Lizzie and I spent our weekends in the country, near where Billy's family lived, with Daddy and Margaret – the pretty Dutch woman, our au pair who graduated to become Daddy's new wife. He continued to treat her like a servant and she seemed to like that, or accept it at least. I think Billy had some powerful feelings about Margaret too – he sorted of wanted to rape Daddy through Daddy's women. A sentiment I admired.

'We would go to the pub in the village which was halfway

between our house and Billy's, meet up with some friends. Go back to our place, swim in the pool – it was the most heated pool in the area, kept at a steady eighty-seven degrees, which made Billy's father crazy with jealousy . . . How on earth can that Blade fellow afford to keep it that warm? It was that kind of petty county scene. They would go into Daddy's bedroom, still wet from the pool, and do it.

'Billy was mean to her. He didn't know what to do with the fact that she was absolutely his. He had no idea, I mean no idea at all, about how to receive her everything. I know he slept with other girls. With her best friend. And then with her second-best friend. He treated her as disposable. She was lovely, wild. She was fourteen years old.

'Billy's parents decided Lizzie and I were dangerous. Between them, his father and Daddy set up a Montague/Capulet scenario which only intensified the relationship for Lizzie. I often wonder whether their coupling merited the force of feeling which was imposed on it from the outside by our disapproving parents.

'Anyway, they forbade the two of them to see one another alone together. Billy and Lizzie met up at the houses of friends or arranged secret assignations on the village common. I acted as a go-between, the guardian angel of their affair.

'Lizzie gave him a bracelet. She had a set of six of them, designed so that when they were worn together they looked like one wide silver bracelet rather than six thin ones sitting close to one another. By giving Billy one she broke the set, sharing it.

'Daddy saw it on his wrist one day and went batshit. The set had been a gift from him – sterling silver. He pulled the bracelet from Billy's wrist, scraping the skin off the back of Billy's thumb in his eargerness to strip him of the fatherly gift. Later, Lizzie gave it to him again. That was how it was. Ours was a tight, small circle.

'I remember it as a summer thing, but maybe memory always reschedules past events to the most appropriate season. Midnight dips, the smell of mown grass, hayfever, the sound of cricket commentary in a next-door room.

'In the middle of that summer – was it midsummer's night? – the three of us went to a black-tie party. For some reason, this was permitted on the condition that Billy had us home by midnight. He borrowed a car from a friend and, having disregarded Lizzie throughout the party, took us home to Daddy bang on time. Daddy found Billy easier to accept in a black tie. If he had known how fast Billy had driven to get back by midnight and how stoned he was – Well, Billy was a bit of a waster: most of the time he wore a Grateful Dead T-shirt, shoulder-length hair, suede platform boots. Very seventies, and in a permanent state of mourning for the late sixties which, by an accident of birth, he had just managed to miss.

'Daddy had his secretary ring Billy once and summoned him to an appointment. Took him into the drawing room: the lecture was about dope – we were smoking a lot of it. Billy expected there to be some mention of the fact that he was clearly schtumping my fourteen-year-old twin sister. But Daddy never mentioned it. Perhaps he didn't believe that they were actually doing it. Perhaps he didn't care. Perhaps we were too young to understand that by lecturing Billy on one type of transgression Daddy was also giving him a message about another.

'Billy always proclaimed that he liked Daddy. He was strangely, perversely determined to win Daddy's approval. He said he felt that he and Daddy were virtually the same person and any differences between them were reconciled in their shared affection for Lizzie. I think the weed was getting the better of Billy's intellectual capacities.

'At the peak of it all, he went on holiday with his parents and his brother. Lizzie and I stayed in England. In Greece, Billy chased a girl who wouldn't let him take her knickers off. He water-skied every day. The girl he was chasing, he was really after her friend but he didn't think he would be able to score with the friend, so he went for the girl he wanted less. That's always been his habit. He even says that throughout the Lizzie thing the person he really wanted was me. Which is bollocks. But anyway.

'Billy stayed up all night eating Morning Glory seeds. His dad was having some sort of breakdown, not helped by the fact that he was spending every waking moment drowning in the electric sauce. Billy couldn't have cared less. He was ashamed of his father's helplessness, felt humiliated by it. His brother was having an affair with an older Greek woman. He swam out to her yacht in the bay. Their parents were getting up for breakfast as Billy and David were coming home to sleep.

'Lizzie bought him a present to welcome him home – a copy of Carole King's *Tapestry*. He repaid the gift by avoiding her.

'I bumped into Billy at a party in London about a year later. It was only then – he still swears that this is the truth – that he discovered what had happened during his absence in Greece. At first I wouldn't talk to him. I was too angry. He was confused: we had become good friends in a conspiratorial sort of fashion. I look so like Lizzie that he must have felt as though it was her who was rebuffing him. Why was I cold-shouldering him? He was out of his depth at the party, a smarter crowd than he was used to, one in which – strange as it may now seem – I mingled with confident ease. He cornered me.

'I told him that the abortion had happened while he was on holiday. I assumed that he had known of Lizzie's pregnancy and simply run away from it. I eventually believed him when he insisted that he was hearing of it from me for the first time. When he asked, as every bloke in that situation does ask, whether Lizzie was sure that the child was – had been – his, I turned my back on him.

'He was being typically male in trying to buck the responsibility. He could only assume that the dead child had been his. He continued to avoid Lizzie, but he and I – who had a number of London friends in common – kept in touch.

'The murdered foetus haunted me. A girl. Dark, in my dreams. Three or four years old. She was stuck in some sort of purgatory. In the dreams I was both myself and the little girl, down in the black place, looking up at the world through a drainage grille, too high above me to reach, the light coming down in barred shafts, a glimpse of a tree, feet rushing past, a cloud crossing the sun. Then the rumble of distant water. I ran along the giant drain, looking for a way out. A tide of waste swept over me and instead of drowning I would wake.'

As I whispered Maria fed me prickly pears, chilled from the fridge, an orange which she divided into segments and biscuits which she broke for me, placing pieces in my mouth.

She led me back to the beach. I carried my clothes in a bundle. I clasped her to me, then set out across the sand.

Instead of dropping, as it sometimes does in the evening, the wind has become stiffer, bustling through the hotel grounds, shaking the electric light through the trees, howling in the power lines, promising some climax that does not arrive. The big wind of calamities, when tempers snap. I have remained on the terrace while Dario and Didier go down to supper. Franz's tower is now illuminated. I see the grotesquely swollen and distorted shadows of his movements on the ceiling of his turret room, a mad scientist awaiting thunder and lightning. He will draw down Zeus's bolts from the air and jolt a new creature into life. When he violates his monster with consciousness, will he be able to contend with the thing he has unleashed?

I contemplate his immaculate hotel, with its shelved lavatories and fastidious landscaping. I think of the stool chart – one of the few areas in which I have permitted my imagination to play. Monday: nine-inch curled worm, good consistency, odour pleasant, pink. Tuesday: brackish effusion, no definition, diesel odour. Wednesday: a fully formed elf with a green felt hat—

The wind is ruffling the bay and out on the far point the breaking waves burst white in the last of the light. A yacht is motoring in from the channel for shelter. There will be no fishing tonight.

A speedboat darts across the bay from the beach, heading for the hotel. I stroll across the terrace to look down at the jetty. The swollen shadows on the turret-room ceiling are juddering about in agitation. The boat approaches fast and seems to be too close to the jetty when the driver cuts the engine and glides towards the dock. A figure jumps from the bow and loops the painter around a post.

The wake of a big ship long passed in the channel has rippled its way to the shore, bumping the speedboat against the dock. A woman stands in the boat, struggling for balance. Her hair is dragged across her face by the wind. She pulls the veil away, to speak. Each time her hand gathers her hair to reveal her face, the wind sweeps it back again.

Surely, it is Lizzie.

At last.

The wind will rise and rise. There will be no storm, no release. The babbling of water and leaf, the howl in the gust-filled wires, the cacophony of music and chatter carried from the bar at the top of the hill, will swirl and swirl. Imagine the responsibility. The precipitations and coincidental collapses. The collisions. In other times they would have burned me. Darker and wiser times.

I am more than simply in control. The extent to which I am out of control has spilled on to those around me to such a degree that I am left immaculate, in white socks and patent-leather shoes, my uniform ironed, my homework completed, neatly arranged in my folder, not an inkstain or a single correction in evidence.

Once a fridge door is open it's hard to close. I've always found that. A tall fridge with a door that unsticks as you pull it open. A fridge with a latch like this one. You pull the chrome handle and it comes away a little at the bottom, a lever lifting inside. I have been in institutions where they keep the fridge locked. Oh yes, and the larder. Here, it is the tower which is locked. The tower.

I have been buried under Daddy's ramparts, and perhaps it is he who watches me from the tower. Does he telephone Franz, demanding updates? What's she doing? Is she safe? Has she lost weight? Has she done anything awful? Will my little girl be all right? Will my little Laura come back unscrambled, unravelled, clear-skinned, reassembled, without that tightness across her cheeks from straining to have the right face to the world?

Those are some of the things he'd want to know; if he were alive; if he wanted to know.

Under the ramparts. Dust to dust. Where the rats scratch at the coffin, scenting not death but the corruption of flesh, their wet noses pressed against the rotting wood, sharp teeth searching for purchase.

I've been so good, Daddy. Losing all my blubber. Such a good girl. Doing what she's told. All lean and lithe and golden. Just the girl a daddy would be proud to call a daddy's girl. Nearly as thin as Lizzie.

I had a jolly good munch in front of the fridge. Only Dimitris pleading to lock up and go home forced a conclusion to my gluttony. A square foot of moussaka, four stuffed tomatoes, three loaves of bread with salt, a litre of yoghurt and honey, twenty-three stuffed vine leaves, six bars of milk chocolate and a partridge in a pear tree. An ample sufficiency, washed down with illicit local wine.

Nick McDowell

That should keep me grounded for a while, I thought to myself, heading for my part of the compound in the big wind.

How could I be so gross? What made me suppose that I could simply enjoy the food? But, then again, why on earth not? Are you all right?

Just a little full, that's all.

That was disgusting.

I can't help it if you don't like it. It's not disgusting to me. It's delicious.

I could not face my little room. Nor could I persuade the candle to stay alight out on the terrace where, despite the sheltering bamboo, the wind gusted, shook the flame and stretched it horizontal until it died. I settled for the meagre reassurance of the orange glow from the tip of my mosquito coil and the familiarity of Brigitte keening next door.

Air gurgled deep in my gut.

My room – God, I miss Lizzie. Oh Christ, I miss her—

My room is halfway up the hill. A number of the residents have to pass by my terrace to reach their own. I am hemmed in by the fact that someone might walk past the bamboo screen at any moment. Even with the wind rattling everything, I fear that someone passing by will hear my every movement.

I light a cigarette and as I inhale I have the sensation of being a fruit, slowly peeled by each intake of smoke. Stop breathing. Doesn't help. An orange. Once I'm peeled, big clumsy hands will divide me into segments, pull away the threads of white inner rind and I will be crushed, burst open by giant ivories.

I can't stand this bamboo enclosure, this Japanese prisoner-of-war camp. Heaving myself out of the wicker chair in which I have been slumped, I plunge inside my

• 178

hut, holding my belly to keep it steady. I genuflect by the bowl, jab fingers at the back of my throat. Nothing.

Not a squirt. Like an engine that won't start in the cold. So I turn the ignition key again. Jab, jabbing the delicate tissue at the back of my throat, begging my gut to heave.

The engine fires and a hot lumpiness gushes on to my hand before I can slip it out of my mouth.

There will be more, but I'll save it up till later. I don't want to spend all my fun at once.

Another cigarette in the grim enclosure, bamboo clicking in the wind like a mad typist, cigarette burning down too quickly from my hungry puffing and the wind harrying.

What could be better than this?

A game of Scrabble, a fuck, an hour or two of channel-switching, people who cared enough to listen, who would actually listen and understand, who would hear.

Or takeaway:

Two cheeseburgers, nine nuggets, large fries – no, make that two large fries – three portions of spring rolls and a gallon of 7-Up to go. Thank you.

Grilled pork dumplings, seaweed, sesame prawn toast, chilli-fried prawns in ginger sauce, shredded beef, wind-dried duck, drunken prawns and Singapore-style noodles. To go. To go.

If Lizzie were here.

To speak, to listen.

We spoke in the same voice. They could not tell our voices apart. Nor even distinguish our faces one from the other. They wished it had been me who died, not her. And I wished it too.

We spoke in the same voice and listened to one another with an ear that no other could offer. When we are separated we are useless. I've looked for her in the strangest places. At the Met in New York, in Joy Fairweather, in Billy, in Daddy, in Maria and, most ludicrously of all, in Mummy. I may yet look for her in Dario where there is not even a stain of her as there is in some of the others, a scent of her to remind me. I thought I could smell her sometimes on Billy. Perhaps I could.

The worst thing is still being able to see her in Mummy – the eyes (with Mummy's loose creased skin subtracted), the chin (but unlined) and a gesture of the hands (holding her palm down by her side, clenching and unclenching her fist) which she did and Mummy still does. Recognising her in Mummy and then shivering at Mummy's chilly otherness.

Intuiting that I minded her having Daddy in a way that I did not, Lizzie offered me Billy as a substitute. He had served as her stand-in, so why not mine? But Billy spurned Lizzie as she was deciding to deny herself the pleasure of him in giving it to me. Nor would she have lost anything by the gift. Lizzie felt what I felt, Lizzie knew what I knew. A taste in Lizzie's mouth was a tang in mine. When there was love in my heart Lizzie shared it. Lizzie wept and my throat would tighten, never mind if she was sitting beside me or on another continent. When a limb is lost the sensation of the limb remains, the feeling of left-legginess, the itch under the arch of the foot. These things last much longer than the amputated flesh. She can probably hear this terrible wind.

Daddy loved Lizzie more than he loved me. I did too. But I couldn't understand that he saw us as different people. We didn't see each other as in the least separable. Why would he want something of her and not want it equally of me? Why would he love Lizzie in one way and me in another? I was utterly perplexed.

Once I had him completely to myself I only missed the Lizzie he was missing and missed her even more than he did, so I couldn't bear to be with him any more than he with me. Hoping I might have it all, I ended up with less than nothing, less than that with which I had started out. Which process of disillusion led me to the consolations of a person such as Vivian.

*   *   *

Can you keep a secret?

Why do these moments of clarity have to be bought at such a high price? The market in lucidity is steeply inflationary.

One nudge from the tip of my forefinger and the regurgitative device roars into life. I grab my hand away quickly and spurt more of my late supper into the bowl. Let's hope I'm puking out the Daddy incubus with the food. I'll try saying something again soon. See if he's gone.

They have compared it to orgasm. There is, of course, a release involved, followed by a limpid mixture of pleasure and loss. A male sort of coming, perhaps, jetting stuff out. But not sexual. Not a bit.

On nights like this I usually paint. In the hospital that was allowed. They decided that if I could stay alert through the Thorazine and the Mellaril, the Haldol and the Largactil, then the painting might at least absorb my attention and stop me pressing the buzzer which disturbed them in the nurse's station. The only drawings I have done here have been on sand.

The wind will not drop. I am still very full of food. The cigarettes taste wrong, as though someone has injected them with chemicals. I pull on a cardigan, not even attempting to button it over my binge-pregnant belly.

15

Walking up the path, I catch a glimpse of Bruce/Daisy on his/her terrace, dancing, twirling about and about. I used to do that. You go on and on until you fall over. Then you lie on the ground, usually with your head singing from the bump it got as you fell, and watch the world go round and round. Then you feel sick. Then you are sick.

No lights or sign of life in Dario's enclosure. I reach the top of the path where I can look down, over the roofs of the hotel, the bamboo fences and cactus hands and olive branches, to the rocks and the water. Behind me is the high fence and beyond it a donkey, standing beside its saddle under a eucalyptus tree.

I squat down, knees apart, belly distended and drooping close to the ground. A squaw preparing for childbirth. I am on a level with the control turret in the top of Franz's tower. He's in there, behind the mosquito screens, shutters still open.

My hands brush the hard ground on either side of my thighs. On an instinct, I glance down. A small white scorpion, three inches from my left foot, almost luminous, flexes its articulated tail, pincers offering a hug. A great surge of wind brings me words:

'—allow me some privacy, for Christ's sake—'
'—beyond which I will not tolerate—'
'—think I should have to put up—'

'—things which from your experience you have no knowledge—'

I cannot look up. I am doing what I can to pin the scorpion to the ground with my stare. This beast is an antenna, relaying radio signals from the tower.

Time passes.

Footsteps close by. The scorpion makes a dash along the path, through the fence.

Could I have dreamt Maria's voice in the tower? How much time has passed?

Here she is now, her hand dropping on to my shoulder.

'Let me take you back to your room, Laura.'

'There was a scorpion.' Shocked into speech by the touch of her hand.

My own voice – not just a whisper. Mine again.

'I want to go home,' I said, still testing it. 'I want my sister.' He must have left with the scorpion. I should have crushed it. But they are sacred like cows in India.

After I refused to get up, after she tried dragging me to my feet, after she cried and told me how tired she was, I forced her to relent. Now I am lying on the bed in her hut at the hotel, watching her pour tea into small Chinese cups. Her head is bent down between me and the candle, light filtering through her hair where it hangs close to the steam rising from the spout of liquid tinkling into the delicate cup.

She has changed into a dressing gown. When she bends again to pour the second cup I can see the shadows opening from her throat to her cleavage, a glimpse of her breasts hanging free within the material. Lovely Maria with her long black hair and her trim form, her wide mouth and swollen lower lip, her narrow ankles and wrists.

When Daddy's mother came to stay, he would barely kiss us goodnight. He and Mummy would not disclose the secret of the unforgivable offence which Granny had committed by the very act of setting foot in the country. Lizzie and I always sided with Granny – Abella, as we called her: our three-year-old stab at Isabella – sympathising with the jilted guest, the innocent elder. We betrayed Mummy cheerfully: no, she doesn't feed us properly; she never reads to us at night; doesn't cook for Daddy; sits and stares out of the window. She hits us, oh yes.

All lies, but approximating to some truth that we were too young to voice. That my mother is a fish did not seem a fact that should be concealed from a paternal grandmother who brought dolls and panforte and chunks of volcanic lava from Italy. Her being a devil to my parents made her all the more our angel. Her embrace, as endless and warm as we wanted it to be, was in such contrast to Mummy's fluttery nervous clutch – Mummy's hugs which ended just before we wanted them to, rejecting our claims upon her with a tiny but undeniable push.

How can he have had such a mother and married such a wife? John Blade, you did but little know yourself. Retreating from a mother who saw your wife as a reptile, and a wife who thought your mother a witch, you ran into the arms of your daughters.

You sought in your twin daughters the thing that neither your mother nor your wife were permitted (in Granny's case) or able (in Mummy's) to offer.

There, you see? I know exactly what's been going on. Don't think I don't.

Maria sips her tea, sitting upon the low stool beside the bed. When I reach out my hand she takes it.

'Tell me a story.'

'I know only Greek stories.'

'Let's have one of those.' I close my eyes, the better to let her voice merge with other voices, the better to suspend the sense of Lizzie's absence. Here is the scorpion, as clear and close as if it had been inscribed in fluorescent paint on the inside of my eyelids. Sepulchral white.

'This is the story of Pallas and Athena,' Maria begins. 'One of many stories about them.'

'I know those names from the hoardings at Piraeus.' I want Maria closer to me but I know I am going to have to be sick again and really quite soon. I'm sure my breath smells foul and sewerish. I don't want her getting a whiff of that and being repelled. Yet I would like her to be unrepellable. I want to feel that slimness about her, each of us incomplete without the other.

So long as she does not speak (with her sweet Greek lispy accent which softens the bonier sounds of English) I am able to make her become the person she so much resembles. But now I have encouraged her to tell me a story. Every time she opens her mouth the spell will be broken, like hugging a velvet cushion and finding it stuffed with barbed wire and broken glass.

I yank my hand from hers and rush to the bathroom, lunging towards the bowl. Just in time. A long, open-throated, gut-bursting shout into the porcelain grave which leaves me panting, gasping for air. She is behind me, her hand on my back, cooing in Greek. I hate her having to smell that smell.

I am so much a lavender person. I am clean and scented, but I keep being caught smelling of chunder and smoked fish. Sometimes the pores of my skin emit the urinous smell of unventilated old stone, of sealed passages below the ramparts.

What am I supposed to do? How do you get close to a person? Dignify them with your desire, flatter them with the lust they arouse in you? That's a short cut. But the other way, the true way, takes so long and is full of obstacles. The road-blocks of terror, that awful terror that you might tell someone how much you adore them and find them blushing in response, turning to stone, freezing over like Mummy does, icicles distending from her nose and earlobes.

Or my adoration might be thought disingenuous, a play designed to gain ground, to contrive me some centrality in Maria's heart which, after all, I simply do not deserve.

A cicada kicks into action somewhere up the hillside, the sound carried on the wind, a generator engine, powering God knows what.

The world looks different seen from this perspective. Like what tramps say about watching from a chilly doorway while humanity hurries home. The porcelain, which was always so chilly and shiver-making at school, is tepid here in Greece. I have no choice but to inspect my outpourings on the shelf provided for stool analysis. The coolest anything gets here is tepid. I used to like the coolness of the porcelain under my chin as my head lolled against the rim of the bowl. That coolness was a place in which I could think clearly, in which I could plan my next move. Right now, I need to make a tactical retreat. But from what, and towards what haven, is hard to say. Pallas is a cigarette brand. Athena is a poster shop. We've raped the past and whatever grandeur once resided in it we've eroded with misuse.

As they have betrayed you, these translators of myth into marketing, so I have betrayed you, lied to you, misled you.

And yet everything I have said to you is true. Do you see the distinction? Sometimes I have to play around with the facts to make the sensations, the truth of what I remember, stand out clearly. Try to understand. It is never a case of what happened but what we remember.

If only the past was a country and we could close the borders for ever.

And yet without it, outside it, we are nothing.

I have attempted to evacuate everyone from my embassy in the past. Do you remember the hands reaching out to the last helicopter off the roof of the American Embassy in Saigon? It's a little like that.

There is nothing I wish to bring out of there, nothing

I want to inherit, no one I need. I am a stand-alone item, a free-standing display-piece. Admire, if you will, my uprightness.

Try to forget, if you can, the image of a frightened girl crumpled in supplication before a lavatory (with double-speed flush and inspection shelf). Frightened because I know what I'm going to do. I know what happens next.

I speak into the bowl, like someone talking into an inverted megaphone:

'You should have met my father. You would have liked him. And he would have liked you. Very much indeed. I'm glad he's not here because he would have liked you better than he ever liked me and then I would have been jealous of you and that would have put me in the same camp as Franz. The wrong camp. Do you know that Franz takes photographs of you?'

Maria's strength surprises me as she heaves me to my feet and turns me around. It is because I am expecting a comforting embrace that the slap catches me unawares, snapping my head back, unbalancing and dumping me on to the loo like someone desperate to open her bowels.

I have taken Maria for a hugger rather than a hitter. You can never tell with these Mediterranean types. All from the African, if Vivian is to be believed, which explains why they are so volatile and tricky. Not that I think of it like that. Oh no. I'm the lavender girl, remember? A nice girl. Daddy's girl.

'You're none of you proper Greeks, are you? Not a trace of nobility left to share out between you. Peasants and shepherds polluted by Turkish blood. I'm surprised Franz will have anything to do with you. Mongrel. Aberration. Thank you.

'And don't try to fool me with the I-slapped-you-to-bring-you-to-your-senses tack. I'm no fool, you know. Not just some bloody fool. No.'

But then I am hugging her, Goddamit. Maria standing

over me, me hugging her around the waist, my cheek pressed against her pubis where I can feel heat and a slight dampness against my skin. I have a good grip on her.

'Let me tell you the story,' Maria says. 'But first, let go of me.'

I can feel a slight swivelling in her pelvis, a moving pressure against my cheek. Why should I let her go? I'll crawl inside her, tube myself up and live off her blood, curled in a ball, gargling amniotic brine, silenced, shrinking all the while until the moment when the blip that was me disappears from the scan and I particulate into sperm and egg, some of me squirming into Daddy, the rest folding back into Mummy's ovary. They could tell me I was falling apart and without fear of contradiction.

The wind is an overloaded aeroplane, whooshing about above us, trying not to fall out of the sky. A reminder of other souls in peril. It threatens to tear the power lines from their masts, to whisk the bay into a dance of white froth.

'Can we go out into the air?' I ask. 'Where I don't have to smell myself.'

'You still have your arms around me.'

'Hit me again,' I say. 'Then I'll let you go.'

'The way you speak of yourself,' Maria says. 'Sometimes it makes me crazy.'

I release her from my clasp.

'Let's go and smoke cigarettes in the wind.'

She led me to a bulging outcrop of rock along the hillside from her room. In front of the bulging rock and immediately below it was a drop to the next terrace. To the side there was a sheer fall down to the sea, the equivalent of a three-floor plunge.

The wind was not cold but it was a third person interjecting himself into our conversation, an unpredictable, interrupting presence. When the force and timing of the waves down below was just right, the water struck the rocks with a delicious crump of broken will. The sea was a demolition gang, hammering away at the wall of rock; the cicadas a pool of mad typists in demonic fugue.

We were a long way from the flat roof outside the dormitory in the Hampshire boarding school where Lizzie and I smoked midnight Woodbines. And yet, of course, as I have been trying to explain, we were in the very same place.

Wrapped in our blankets, heads full of Herman Hesse and Mervyn Peake, at fifteen we were able to have late-night conversations which solved everything. We talked for a couple of hours and had it all worked out – religion, meaning, politics, beauty. Because we were reaching ancient conclusions for the first time they had for us the force of newly minted truths.

I mourn the period of my life in which I could read a book like *The Glass Bead Game* or *The Rainbow* and experience revelation. Ah, now I understand. So that's what it's all about. Now I know how to be. Or *Crime and Punishment*. Or *L'Etranger*.

Live by the book, if you must. But die by it.

'I'm sorry, Maria. Truly.'

She was on the exposed side of the bulging rock, sitting cross-legged, head bent forward, hair hanging across her face. When she caught it back behind her ears it would hang there only to slip back over her face again a moment later. The girl in the boat. Exposed to the three-floor drop, to the wailing turbines of the wind, to the conversation of Laura Blade, painter, fantasist, sometime hang-glide historian and problem eater.

Maria took the offered cigarette. We struggled to light up, huddling together, Kent and Edgar cupping our hands around a series of guttering matches.

Lizzie had a Zippo which Billy had given her. She liked windy nights on which we could demonstrate its efficiency.

'Athena', Maria began, her features illuminated by the glow of her cigarette, 'was born from the head of Zeus. She cracked her father's skull open in order to enter the world. She arrived, causing her father great pain, fully formed in miniature. She spent her childhood in Africa—'

All from the African, just like Viv said.

'—where Zeus appointed Triton as her guardian. Triton's daughter was called Pallas. She was the same age as Athena. They were like sisters. More than that. They looked so very alike that they were mistaken for one another, even by Triton as he watched over them in the subtle African twilight. People supposed they were twins. Only by the hard light of noon could you tell that Pallas was darker than Athena—'

Lizzie had betrayed me. But I – storyteller supreme – had saved my large-breasted sister from the torment of our schoolmates. The heavy breasts and narrow waist that Billy liked so much, that Daddy found so enticing. I have the same waist, but my breasts are smaller.

'The daughters of Zeus and Triton played together all day. Left to themselves as they grew older, they indulged their imaginations, playing out the battle tales Triton had told them at bedtime. They fashioned their own weapons and as they developed in strength and stature, their fights became more violent—'

The trouble with having a sister who is almost you is that, while she is your lifetime companion and friend, she is also your rival. People can't help it, they choose between you, favouring one above the other.

'One day the sparring girls had a particularly brutal battle. Watching them from Mount Olympus, Zeus feared for Athena's safety—'

Lizzie and I squatted on the flat roof outside the dorm. She told me she had let them kill her child. Had said, yes, all right then, do it. Having the baby, she said, would have ruined her. But I've killed a part of myself, she kept saying.

Why would I want to go on living, now that I've killed that part of me? What would be the point?

Didn't Lizzie realise I'd heard enough? That I wanted her to just shut up?

'To protect his child, Zeus angled his sword so that the light of the sun dazzled Pallas. Athena, too engaged in the fight to hold back, thrust her spear into the heart of her blinded friend—'

What else could I do? I kept thinking that Lizzie would realise in time that it was just too provocative, that I couldn't hear any more. She squatted there on the flat roof, banging on about her dead child – as if I wasn't even there – talking out into the night, puffing away at her cigarette. Pretending to me that the child had been Billy's when we both knew perfectly well whose child it had been. Mummy knew. Margaret knew. Even Billy worked it out in the end.

'Athena made a wooden statue of her dead friend. She would dress and undress the effigy, giving it a daily routine. Like a child mothering its doll. When she looked at the effigy, she had the sensation that she was looking at her own reflection in a pool. Had she killed herself, she wondered, when she burst Pallas's heart with her spear?—'

I hardly thought about it, just reached out and gave Lizzie a little shove with the flat of my right hand. As she fell the three floors to the ground I realised that I had been wanting to do it for ages. I was liberating her. Letting her off the hook. I finished my cigarette before climbing back through the window into the dormitory and sounding the alarm. If I didn't have to carry her weight, I'd float away, light as anything.

'Later a monster – also called Pallas – tried to rape Athena. She killed the monster and stripped its skin with a knife. She became a great slayer of men and monsters. But the only killing over which she suffered any remorse was that of her childhood friend, her twin, her mirror-image.'

When I reached out for Maria she was no longer cross-legged beside me but standing with her back against the wall of rock, braced against the threat of the wind gusting and toppling her down on to the rocks below. So frail and thin and pretty. And pleased with her little ploy. Her apposite myth. Reading my case-notes. Making her assessment.

You will recall the list of traitors in my story to date – Tartan Diana, Billy, Rae-Ann, Lizzie, Vivian, my parents, Franz, Joy Fairweather. Even Margaret, adopting herself into the family, committed a form of treachery, submitting to the lure of Daddy's bed, abandoning me in the process. And now Maria.

'So Lizzie's dead.' My voice was deep again. My deep Daddy voice. 'Who gives a fuck?'

'You have insisted that she is alive.' Maria stood closer to me now, directly behind me. I felt her kneecaps touch my shoulder-blades. 'Why?'

'She's alive,' said my baritone. 'Daddy's a ghost. I'm a ghost. You're a ghost.'

'She jumped,' Maria said. 'You were at home with glandular fever. You weren't there. Say it. Say – I wasn't there. She killed herself.'

'No.'

'Lizzie jumped,' Maria said. 'You weren't even there.'

'I killed her.'

'She left a note. You know it off by heart.'

'No,' I said.

'She committed suicide,' Maria said. 'You felt guilty that you had been ill. You think you could have saved her. She jumped from the roof and broke her neck. Say it. Know it. It is the truth.'

Well, you know what I feel about factual truth.

Twisting my torso, I grabbed Maria's legs in a rugby tackle and shoved her off balance. Her head bounced on rock with a sharp crack. I disentangled myself from her slack limbs and rolled her over the edge.

No, I said to myself, in my best Daddy voice. She jumped.

I took a last drag from my cigarette, flicked the stub into the night and looked down to the rocks below.

Is that Lizzie or Maria down there, looking all crumpled and broken, or just some child's doll brought ashore by the big wind?

It should have been Daddy, of course. If Edgware hadn't failed me. If Vivian hadn't betrayed me.

You can't trust anyone these days, can you?

16

Vivian Black

'I want my phone call,' I said. 'It's the law you give me my phone call.'

'What would you need with a solicitor?' the detective asked. 'If you haven't done anything wrong.'

'That's right,' I said. 'So what the fuck am I doing here smoking your fags?'

'You're small-time, Viv.' The detective flicked through the file in front of him. 'Mean. But small.'

Not falling for that one. 'I like to leave the heavy stuff to those what—'

'What heavy stuff, Viv?' The detective pushed his cigarettes and lighter closer to me again.

They ain't charged me yet, which could be a good sign. I don't know what the fuck to watch out for. Laura? The kids? Edgware? They don't hold you for questioning cos you fell over in the street made a git of yourself. Fat chance.

Wish I knew what happened to that motor. Hope they ditched it like I told them. And Edge – wonder whether he made it. It's not just the confinement, see, it's the way all the things you care about in the world just stop dead. Like a power cut. Don't find out what happened sometimes till years later by which time who gives a bollocks, frankly?

And no nookie.

'What heavy stuff?'

'Proper crimes,' I said. 'You know.'

'You don't count rape as a proper crime, Viv? Or take kidnap. Now, there's a crime I'd take very seriously indeed. Or shooting people. Shooting people is a serious business. Can't be too careful who you shoot, can you?'

'That's right,' I said.

'You got a habit, Viv?' The detective lifted the cuff of my shirt to clock me forearms.

'Not me, squire.'

'Use a bit of gear, set you up, now, couldn't you?'

'Don't touch the stuff,' I said. 'Got me into too much trouble, that did.'

'True enough, Viv,' the detective said. 'True enough.' They pay these blokes to detect, to observe, right? But I never come across one had a decent tie. This one he has post-box red with a pale blue stripe.

'Evidence. Keep it locked up down the corridor. Bags and bags of the stuff. Gets lost all the time. Pills, powders, ampoules. Funny, that.'

'The phone call.'

'You still put it about a bit, don't you, Viv?' The detective lit a fag. 'A bloke like you. In his prime.'

'I'm a married man, me.'

'Your missus would be very, very upset she heard the half of what you get up to.' He stood up. 'Tell me about it, Viv. Man to man.'

'It's personal.'

'It's personal when you give a bird one, is that right?'

'It might be.'

'You give a bird one and it just so happens she don't want it, that's very personal indeed, wouldn't you say?'

'Depends.'

'You give her one up the arse when she don't want it, begging you to stop, she is' – leaning over me, his boat up to mine – 'fighting you, scratching, maybe, screaming, so you clamp your hand over her mouth. Now surely that's personal.'

'Yeah.'

'And if you come—' He sat down and smiled at me. 'Well, that's a little cupful of evidence you left behind, isn't it? Wasn't it?'

'It's unnatural.'

'It's illegal, son.' The little fucker. 'Even between husband and wife. Trouble is, a woman she has a bit of pride, she doesn't much feel like taking the witness box and describing it to the court: Then he forced entry into my rectum. I was screaming. Then he hit me. Then he pushed it in further. And did you try to stop him? asks the defence lawyer – your lawyer, Viv, and I hope they give you a good one. You have to imagine being the victim. Can you do that?'

'— '

'The defence lawyer, who might even be a woman too, gives the impression that you didn't try hard enough to stop this drugged-up thug who had you pinned against the bath from stuffing himself up your bum. Suggesting that actually, given the chance, you'd go out in the street, grab the nearest bloke, and ask him to do exactly that. Now that is what I call personal.'

'I want my phone call.' He wouldn't see the point if I told him she come. When a bird comes it don't leave no evidence.

'A case of this sort, more often than not, they have to stitch the rectum where it's been ruptured by the entry. And of course, the police photographer has to take shots of all the wounds.' The detective offered me another cigarette. 'Imagine trying to take a shit, Viv. Just imagine.'

I took the fag. He held out the flame, making me lean forward to get it lit.

'There's a WPC at this station. Lovely girl. Could go far. Wants to get into CID. Made it plain to me just how much. What do I do? I could give her one. I've thought about it. Slim little ankles on her, nipples you can see pointing through the bra. Blonde. Educated. My type.

'I could walk her home any day of the week, slip upstairs and have my wicked way. She might even like me, who knows?

'So I have a think about it. But I don't know what to do. I get stiff thinking about it. Wonder if she would suck my dick? What's her cunt like? Is it slick and tight, how we like it? What would you do, Viv?'

'I want to have the phone call what it is my legal right to have.'

'Should I wait until she's begging for it?'

'I don't care about your fucking problems.'

'You could meet her. I could have her in here right now, asking questions. Would you like that?' He went to the door and knocked. 'Or I could send in some of my colleagues from Birmingham who would very much like a word. You have a little think. WPC Collins or the Birmingham murder squad. You have a little think.'

The duty sergeant unlocked the door and let the detective out of the interview room.

Think, Viv, for fuck's sake think. They haven't charged you yet. Fags still on the table. Took a few, popped them in me shirt pocket. Why?

Cos they got no evidence. Or—

They don't know which charge they can most likely get a conviction on. Or—

They want Edgware. If Edgware is alive. Would they know he was hit?

Laura's got the bottle for a court case.

But put her in a courtroom any brief worth his biscuit would discredit her in three minutes. A nutter, plain and simple.

I been through it. It's tough on the bird, even when it's a clear-cut guilty as charged.

That was never rape. Honest. You call that rape? Me, I call it pushing the limits of erotic adventure. The birds and the bees. Nature's way, I reckon she shopped me cos I fucked up her plans to polish off her dad.

Maybe things got out of hand the second time, but she was acting like a cunt and passion is what passion does. You saw it. She never give me respect. Edgware I reckon it is they want. Getting Edgware would be something. If he's alive. Think. Think. Think. Sounds familiar, that does.

Snitch on Edgware, and get off the rape charge. Or risk she won't take the stand.

Then there's the little girls. Is that wot he meant by kidnap? What else? See what the WPC can tell me.

If Edge is dead, that's me fucked. Giving them Edgware has consequences an' all. Like looking over my shoulder the rest of my life. But if it keeps me on the outside.

They'll have to charge me soon.

The WPC took her jacket off, set it on the back of the chair. Bold as brass. Must be twenty-five with a bit of the Swedish in her like that bird what used to do the weather on the telly. Nice knockers. Very nice. But the regulation stockings and them bungey shoes they wear. Spoils it a bit. Don't reckon she'd let that scummy detective anywhere near.

'Help me, Vivian.' The damsel in distress. 'There's something I don't understand.'

'You know my name,' I said. 'But I don't know yours.'

'That's because you are a suspect, Vivian. And I am a police officer.'

'Suspected of what?' I went. 'I ain't done nothing 'cept get legless. We all like to have a good time.'

'At eight in the morning?' That bossy voice like Laura does. All schoolmistressy. Love it. 'You must have had a very good time indeed.'

'What don't you understand?'

'How can you be so stupid?'

'Hold on a minute.'

'No, you hold on, you little bastard. I know that look you're giving me. That target look. I've seen it before. We could convict you even if she didn't take the stand.'

'Bollocks.'

'Let me read you something: 1977 – assault and battery on a nineteen-year-old girl. Three years with remission. I'll miss out the other things you went down for; 1980: attempted rape charge. No conviction—'

'All right. All right.' Look, I can explain all that. The first one they should never of done me. I mean, it was a misunderstanding. The second one they never convicted. It might be in the file, but don't jump to conclusions.

'Confess this and we can make the Birmingham people go away.'

'Bollocks.'

'Don't you want to tell me about it?'

'That 1977—'

'You want to, don't you?'

'Listen a minute.'

'You could try to shock me, telling me all about it. Think about doing it to me as well. That would be exciting, wouldn't it? We could both have a bit of fun.'

'Go on, then. Get the recorder.'

Once they got the machine and witnessed the switch-on I had the others cleared out. She puts the mike in front of me and she's all hotted up cos she thinks she's got me and maybe this will be her chance. Make a case, go for CID.

'I would like to record', I said, 'that this here WPC

who won't tell me her name indicated, in the course of interrogation, that it would give her pleasure to hear me describe a rape which she alleges I committed. I have nothing to add, except that I never done nothing, until my lawyer is in the room. I demand a phone call. I demand you release me or charge me.'

Not a blush. Tougher than what I fancied.

Back in the cell. Still no phone call. Usually they give it about two hours. Let you think about it.

Not much on offer 'cept grassing up Edgware. More I think about that, the less I like it. Protection, that's what I'd need. Twenty-four fucking hours a day. Might not get bail anyway, whichever they charge.

That cunt Laura. I'd like to get my hands on her. Fuck, yes. I'll show her pressing charges. I'll show her fucking witness box.

If I knew about Edgware. If only. Lost a few pints of blood on to the back seat of my motor and no mistake. So much for the plush.

But they can work miracles these days. The Birmingham targets, they was well toasted. Two I saw wasn't never giving no evidence to anyone but their maker. That's two murders.

I'm just the driver. Unless they find the motor. Have they got the motor? The number plate?

Like a game of chess. Pawn to king four.

Let's say I shop him. Then he dies. Perfect.

I never should of clocked her. Never should have told her about Edgware, neither. Never should of interfered.

Shit happens. Most of it seems to happen to me, an all.

I should not be telling you this.

But there's no one else to talk to.

You breathe a word, I'll bite your nipples off.

I mean it. I done it before.

Well, almost.
But seriously. Stay schtum.

It was an Edgware job. He had a contract down in Hampshire. Out on the M3. New Forest. Lovely spot.

Edgware in the back and we was listening to the Test match on the radio. He smells a bit. Feet. So we got the windows open and the radio up high, them old fucks banging on in the tea break about how it was in 1955 when they was sober enough to see the ball.

Pulled up on a little country lane with hedges higher than a man. Edgware put on his mask.

'I'm bringing him out, Viv,' he said.

'You never,' says I, but he drops this wedge in my lap.

Told me to watch for him by the gates round the corner and then he dove through the hedge like a ferret.

Bang out of order. Bringing a target out to my motor. But when I finished counting, I decided eight hundred quid was eight hundred quid. That's always been it with Edgware. Always knew how much wedge was just a bit more than wot I can't say no to. Should call him Wedgeware on account of it.

The end of play. England, 220 for 9. Usual fuck-up. Lucky I support the West Indies. Switched to Radio 1. Watched the gates. Smoked.

Some things I just remember. You know – the way you do. Other things, I think about them, it replays in my head like a tape and I get all the sensations, like it was happening again: instant replay and slow motion. I get that I know I'm remembering something what I shouldn't never of done, and that's what I got now. A stupid thing, but a bad thing 'n' all.

It was getting dark when he walked the bloke out. Three

hours is a long time to wait. For Edgware it's a millennium.

Walked the bloke out but only just, cos he'd worked on him already. Nothing visible, mind, but the target was limping, carrying hisself like a bag of water about to burst. Edge had a pop at his kidney, was my guess.

'Just tell me why.' Target spoke funny, must of lost a tooth or two. Poncy accent with a trace of the foreign. Silk suit.

Edgware not being given to verbal, the dialogue never got started.

'Who asked you to do this?' he goes.

'How much do you want?' he goes.

And so on.

Edge had given me an address before we left town. A school not far from the house where we got the target. I drove there.

It's the holidays, not a soul in sight. Empty playing fields. One of them private schools. Parked up under an oak tree.

'Look, if this is something to do with my children – my child.'

'Shut the fuck up,' I said to the target. 'Cunt.'

Edge knocked in the glass on a door while I held the bloke. Something about his face. I put it out of my mind.

A lot more involved than what I ought to of been. Eight hundred quid. In tenners. Makes a proper wedge in the pocket.

The target started to shudder. He had it bad. Like me with the doctor when Dean said to top him. He give off that smell they have when they know they're for it. Never did like that smell.

Edgware had a floor-plan of the building. He led us through corridors with a torch. Up the stairs to the dormitories. Ten little beds, all in a row. Metal beds, the mattresses doubled back so half the springs showed underneath.

Edgware opened up all the windows. Beckoned me and the target over to a window where there was a flat roof outside. You could get to it if you slipped down the eave below the window.

The worse smell come. The target shit himself. Not getting out of the window. Hollering and screaming. Crying. Begging. Edge taped his mouth.

Oh fuck.

Edgware and me we roped him up, wrists and ankles. Slotted him through the window like posting a letter. Slid him down on to the flat roof. Fag-ends everywhere.

Fuck, fuck, fuck. I never should of. Eight hundred.

The target was on his knees, leaning his head on my thighs. Wonder what the fuck he done to deserve this? I thought.

Edgware got this little red notebook out of his pocket, the sort of notebook a train-spotter might use. Very methodical crim, is our Edge. In capital letters, he had written and now said in a flat voice what made a nonsense of the words: 'If you miss Lizzie that much, follow her where you sent her.'

Edgware was ready to give him the heave-ho. A three-floor drop.

The target looked right confused.

Oh fuck, I thought. Fuck me for being such a stupid cunt.

I pulled the target's wallet from his jacket. Driving licence – John Franco Blade.

'Hold it,' I said to Edge.

He stared at me, cold as death.

'You can't do this.'

'Go back to the vehicle,' he said.

'I said no,' I said to him. 'I fucking mean it.'

'You cunt.' Edgware pulled his shooter.

'Who ordered this?' I asked him.

'Get the fuck out of here.' Edge had his shooter on Blade.

'You don't want this one on your hands.'

'You stupid cunt,' he goes. Edge was gutted. He had reckoned I was sound.

'I'll do you,' he said. 'You seen me do it.'

'Go on, then, you little cunt,' I said to him, I said, thinking, none of this would of happened but for that stupid bit of gash.

Then John Blade nutted Edgware in the bollocks. Edge lost his balance and slipped off the flat roof, sliding down the tiles of the sloped bit. Got his shoes wedged in the gutter.

Now tell me, what the fuck was I supposed to do?

I unroped Blade, helped him back through the window. Untaped his mouth.

'Did he say Lizzie?' Blade asked. He slumped down on the floor. On his side. Still had a dump in his underwear.

'He din say nothing,' I said.

I looked out of the window. Edge was crawling up the tiles, like a crab, his hair out of place; the long bit what he slicks across his bald patch was hanging down the side, right down to his collar.

'You best scarper,' I said to Blade.

I had to help the bastard to his feet and get him down the stairs. Then we only couldn't find the door we come in so I stove in a window in the kitchens and we went out that way.

'Run for it, you fucking nonce,' I said to him. 'Go on. Piss off.'

Then I watched him lollop off across the playing field, him with the dump still in his trousers.

Couple of days later, scrolling through the memory of me car phone, I came to Edgware's number. It hit me like a smack rush.

There she was on the blower in my motor all the time;

all she had to do was scroll the phone memory and there was Edge's number.

I shouldn't of never mentioned Edgware to Laura. I never should of. All mouth, me.

She fucking had it coming, din she? You reckon I was too soft on her? I probly was.

I give her a piece of my mind soon as I got back to town.

'He'll fucking do me,' I said to her.

'Edge don't fuck about,' I said.

Was she sorry?

Was she bollocks.

Slagged me off for interfering.

The nerve of it.

'I should fucking skin you,' I said to her. 'What the fuck's your dad done to you you hate him that much?'

'He's dead already,' Laura goes. 'The rest is technical.'

Technical? Technical? Who does she think she is? Charles Bronson?

I wouldn't let her out the motor till she give me a proper explanation. She tried it all: tears, joking, see if she could get me to fuck her, screaming, hollering, accusing. All the stuff birds do when they don't want to give over.

Then she give up and went quiet.

I asked her again. 'Why'd you ask Edge to top him?'

'You don't want to know.'

'Listen, you stupid slag, you cunt—'

'He fucked my sister.'

That was me told.

'He fucked my sister,' Laura said. 'And he made her pregnant and blamed it on her boyfriend – Billy. Then he forced her to have an abortion.'

Fuck a duck.

'We were only fifteen. Apart from actually pushing her off the roof, he did everything to kill her.'

'Jesus, doll,' I said to her. What can you say? I mean, I was gutted, literally gutted.

'And now he wants to ruin my life, because I wouldn't fuck him. Because I still won't. And because he knows that I know and he's afraid of me. He can't control me.'

Which was a daft thing to say, really, seeing as how she'd just put all of us in the way of attempted murder.

'I only wanted him to love me,' Laura said. 'Like a daddy.'

Eight hundred quid was starting to look too cheap.

Makes you jumpy being on the wrong side of a bloke like Edge. I was waiting for the knock on the door. Praps it's better if the iffy doctor lets him cross the river.

It showed me what can happen if you hang out with nutters.

It showed me what can happen if you mouth off.

So stay quiet, Viv.

Wait till they charge you.

17

'Are you the owner of a black BMW 535 injection. C reg?'

'No.'

'Why's it registered in your name, then?'

'It got nicked,' I said. 'A car like that, everyone wants to get their hands on it, turn into Nigel Mansell. I got a crime reference number.'

This was the Birmingham lot.

'I'll have to fetch that WPC Collins, Viv. Talk some sense into you.' Ha fucking ha.

'I'm a minicab driver.'

'And I'm Ron Atkinson,' said the older detective, the one who looks close to retirement, a copper of the old school (come-on-son-I-know-your-type-give-us-a-name). Understands the villain from spending forty years closer to villains than the upright. More of a villain in his head, you might say, than most villains. Red hair turning grey, makes him look like something the cat dug out the rubbish tip.

'No shooting or possession of firearms on your extensive record,' said Old School. 'Makes lively reading, it does. What a varied life you've had. What a busy fella.'

'I want my phone call.'

'Witnesses say there were two of you in the motor, but we've only got one of you. Blood in the car, blood and fibres. Chunks of flesh on the front bumper – you really should learn to clean up after yourself, a professional like yourself. Steering-wheel prints say Vivian Black woz here. Open and closed. I smell a conviction.'

'I'm a minicab driver.'

'An innocent bystander – that's how I see you, Viv. You drive the car, you don't want to know about the rest of it. More a witness than an accomplice. Could be not much more than dangerous driving you're looking at. But? But but but—'

The kid took over, the raw one with the laptop computer, the baby face:

'We need someone to do the murders. This bears all the signatures of a killer we've been after for—'

'Since you were in nappies,' said Old School, glancing down at the fingers of the raw kid click-clicking at the laptop. 'Funny, that. We've all been in nappies. Even this Vivian here started off on his mother's tit. The milk must have been sour. It got him off to a bad start. Poor little nipper, not getting his proper pint. A feeling of compassion comes over me. I think, this Vivian Black could go away for two murders. Why? Because of some fuzzy idea about honour among thieves which went out with Ealing comedy. The vestiges of an era long gone by.'

'We would put you somewhere safe,' said the raw kid.

'What about the other charges?'

'Not our jurisdiction,' said the kid.

'I want my phone call.'

I want to tell 'em. I need to tell 'em. As if I ain't had a shit in weeks and now I'm ten yards from a khazi but I can't get there. Need a brief keep my mouth shut. Just someone to talk to. WPC Collins. But I fucked that up.

Laura—

I din never mean to hurt her. Honest, I din. Told you what I think about hitting women. I never meant to hit her. Fucking cow pushing me, I mean did she push me or what?

Come on, Viv. Focus.

'I want you out of it,' I said to the kid. 'I'll talk to you,' giving Old School the nod. 'You and WPC Collins. That's it. And no tape. Otherwise, I'll wait for me brief.'

Stupid.

In she come, the changing of the guard. The raw kid all ruffled, carting his computer.

'What's on offer, then?' I asked.

Old School and the weather girl looked at each other. Got them in a muddle.

That's good.

'If you want a royal flush, I want my call. Otherwise, what's the crack?'

'Why should we offer you anything, Viv?' The weather girl, soft-voiced, like we was in the sack. 'What have you given us?'

'It's the brief, then, is it?'

'You little fucker.' Old School lumbered on to his on-the-beat flat feet. 'You little cunt. Excuse me, miss.'

'You like that word, don't you, Vivian?' The weather girl crossed her legs under the table. 'I should think you like to hear a woman saying it. Shall I say it for you?'

Focus, Viv. For fuck sake, focus.

'The identity of the shooter for the rape,' I said. 'Plus whatever else you got.'

'Listen to it, luv,' said Old School. 'He thinks he can give us a name and walk out of here. I've seen villains try it when they're wet behind the ears. Get the scent of freedom in their schnozz, think they can walk away from it all. But an old lag like you, Viv? You should know better.'

Nobody said nothing. Letting that sink in. Tactics, right? Give him hope—

Then plunge him into despair. Up and down and round about.

Fuck that. Let them stew.

It was her calling me Daddy what done it. Got me restless. There she was, all prone in the front seat. Will Daddy punish

me now? Love her like a daughter. Too fucking right.
Straight round to casualty. Get her sorted. Well, almost.
Little detour in there somewhere. After the little girls. Side
street in Little Venice. I never should of. Sheer folly.

A bunch of cunts, the lot of you. Cunts to a man.

Think I can't get out of this one? Just you fucking
watch.

'Let's spose', I said, 'that I know this bloke you think done
the shootings in Birmingham.'

'Who said it was Birmingham?' said Old School.

'WPC Collins' boss,' I said. 'What d'you think I am? A
dickbrain?'

'Calm down, Viv.'

'Let's spose I tell you who he is; where he is. What
then?'

'You take the stand,' Old School said.

'I ain't taking no fucking stand,' said I. 'You got me cos
you got my motor, so you say, which means you must have
a witness for where the motor was, which means you don't
need me in the stand. Am I right?'

'In return,' WPC Collins said, 'you take assault instead of
rape, dangerous driving instead of manslaughter, and the
attempted kidnap disappears. Two years inside.'

'And the rest of my life on the run.'

'It's not supposed to be an easy choice,' said WPC Collins.
'But it is a choice.'

I was ready to give it then. The name – the name of the
man you know as Edgware – already sitting on my tongue
like a big bronchial gob ready to get spat out on the floor.
A gob with a solid string of snot behind it with his address
on it and the address of the iffy doctor.

'You're on,' I said. 'Get the brief in here and we'll do it.'

'Much more complicated like that,' said Old School. 'Let's
just do the business and sort the details after. Isn't that what
you want?'

'Don't tell me what I want,' I said. 'I want my brief and

I want you out of it. You get my brief on the blower. I don't want no legal aid halfwit.' I told him the name and the number.

'And you stay here,' I said to the weather girl. 'I got words I want with you.'

'Well?' she asked once he was out of it.

'Do you enjoy it?'

'Enjoy what?'

'Listening,' I said. 'To confessions.'

'It's part of the job,' she said.

'Must be hard to shut it off just like that.'

'Sometimes it is.'

'I don't care about the rest of it,' I said. 'Do what the fuck you like. One thing I need, though. I need to talk to someone. Off the record.'

'There's a counselling service,' she said. 'Or we can get you a priest. What's your denomination?'

'No,' I said. 'I want you to hear it.'

'Why would I put up with listening to you unless there was a conviction at the end of it?'

'Who said there isn't?' I went. 'Who the fuck said that?'

'Off the record, you said.' She was curious.

'I don't hit women, right?'

She was up out the chair and banging on the door faster than you could say help in Swedish.

'Wait a minute.' They don't understand nothing. 'I gotta talk to you.' The door opened.

'You all right in there, miss?'

'Stay by the door, please. I may need you.' The door closed again. 'I shouldn't be doing this.' She sat down again, scraping the chair-legs against the floor, moving back from the table, away from me.

'That's something we got in common, then.'

'What is it you want to tell me?'

'I done some bad things, right? I know some of them was bad things. But I didn't start off meaning no harm to nobody. Some things I done was business, which is a choice I made. Some things I done for a lark. Some things was for respect. And some things I done, I'm ashamed.

'She wanted it, see? She wasn't wearing no knickers. You got to wear knickers you don't want no one getting inside them, innit?'

'You hurt her,' the weather girl said. 'She was severely concussed.'

'I never,' I said. 'She must of fell over. She wanted it. They all want it if you give them a chance to admit it.'

'I don't want it,' the weather girl said. 'It's the last thing in the world I want.'

'With respect, miss, you don't know what you want.'

'We aren't getting anywhere, are we?'

'Abuse. Some things is just abuse. And that's wrong. I won't have that.'

'Like?'

'Don't get funny,' I said. 'It wasn't random. She's my friend.'

'That's how you treat your friends, is it?'

'I took advantage. She was raving. This is another time. Before the time she says was rape and I say to you she come so it can't be rape.'

'Date?'

'Never you mind. She was raving so I had to hit her. We done something we didn't ought to of done. Almost got nicked. Then she lost the plot. Went nutty on me. Had to clock her to calm her down. The kids was gone by then.'

'I don't think I want to hear this.'

'They never got hurt. Just scared. I wouldn't never hurt a kid. I told her. Then I clocked her. My friend.'

'She's not your friend, Vivian,' said the weather girl, flying straight into the bull's-eye of the web. 'She shopped you for all of it.'

Gotcha.

Used my brain for once.

If Laura told them, then it's all iffy. Do you get it, or what?

'That's as maybe.'

If all they got is Laura's statement.

Fuck me. I could be in clover.

Hang on, son. Stay calm.

'She was passed out in the motor. Nose bleeding. I never should of done it. I mean, is it rape if she's delirious and who knows whether she wanted it or not? My guess, she would of been glad of it.'

'We'd have to ask her.'

'Took her back to her flat, carted her up the stairs over the shoulder. Tucked her up in bed. Tucked her up and got the doctor round to sort her. I wiped the blood off her face. She started to come round. Groggy. Helped her undress. Daddy, I'm tired, she goes. Tuck me up in bed, Daddy. Read me a story.

'Then she touched me. Where I live. No mistaking it.

'Soon enough we was bang at it. Squirming about, she was, delirious, like I said. Daddy this, Daddy that. Just about to come, I am, and she conks out. But I went on, see. She could of snuffed it and I went on just the same. Chucked me mix in. I shouldn't never of done that. That was wrong, plain and simple.'

The weather girl didn't say nothing. I had her wanting the next bit. I had her there with me, thinking about it.

'Time I got her to casualty she was coming round again. Dumped her on a bench and scarpered.'

Collins don't realise what she done. Me, I'm sure they got it all from the mouth of Laura and not much supporting. As witnesses go, she's about as reliable as the weather in April. Collins don't say nothing for a bit. I take a fag out me shirt pocket and gesture for a light. No. She don't have a light.

'You know what I hate about this job?' she said eventually. 'You know what makes me want to give it all up?'

'What's that, then, love?'

'You people do these terrible, unforgivable things—' The
choke in her voice told me she meant the words. 'And then
when we apprehend you, when we've cornered you and
you can't lie or cheat or threaten your way out of it, you
suddenly develop consciences and ask us to feel sorry for
you because you've done things you are ashamed of. I hate
having to listen to you. It makes me feel implicated. But
there's no absolution, Mr Black. And no sympathy. And no
understanding. And you should be ashamed.'

Implicated? Absolution? Too many graduates on the force
these days.

'I acted like a cunt,' I said.

'And you should be treated like one,' the weather girl
said, hearing herself say it, wishing she hadn't, knowing
she couldn't unsay it. Wondering, I reckon, how she got
herself saying a thing like that to a piece of shit like me.

Checkfuckingmate.

'I'm going to hurry your brief along.' She stood and
turned towards the door. A bit of her white shirt-tail had
come out of her skirt at the back and was hanging down
over her bum. Innocence is a beautiful thing. 'I won't forget
you,' she said, knocking on the door.

Said it like lovers do, even if she never meant it that
way. Another young copper with a cause – Vivian Black.
And before I even got round to telling her about the geezer
I creamed.

Back in the cell for an hour.

When my brief come he made me stay schtum. Still no
charges.

They had to let me go. They ran out of time.

Once I was out, I learnt that Laura was on a section order.
Tried to jump off the steeple of a church. Then her dad
carted her off to a nuthouse in the Med. Bucket-and-spade
asylum for the BUPA classes.

What they had was her statement which, once she was
sectioned, must of looked like a string of pork pies.

They never had the car, which was in bits at the breaker's in Penge. I got back the sound-rig and the tapes.

Edgware got sorted by the iffy doctor. Gone into retirement, so he says. We play snooker on Fridays. He's taken to needlepoint. Cushion covers. Funny old world.

Me, I'm a minicab driver. Picked up a diesel Merc in the Old Kent Road. Keep my head down.

Who the fuck do you think you are to judge me? I might have been banged up once or twice, done one or two things I didn't ought to of done, but I'm not a bad man. I know what love is. I know how to treat a person.

Laura got mouthy. Had to be sorted. But I love her. Like a daughter.

And why the fuck shouldn't I walk the streets like the next man? Where's the evidence? Don't believe everything you hear. There's people about, want to pull the wool. Make you believe things aren't the way they are.

So back off.

I mean it.

18

Franz Marelli-Kreitznacht

Michaelis, can you the nerve of it believe? Maybe it is time for a new guide.

What is it in you, Michaelis said, which chose for this to happen.

In me?

Choice?

You should laugh that I choose such a man to ask me such questions. And pay him to ask. Trying to tell me I had done this to myself. The same thing he said of Helga when she tried to steal the house from me. Also, when the Americans tried to freeze the assets of the Florida Institut.

Now that was a woman again, he said. As if in this he had the second law of thermodynamics discovered. Natalie Spode of the Inland Revenue Service. Eat the faeces of your mother in hell, Natalie.

The final gall was when he said to me: Just suppose that you had chosen your parents. What would it mean to make such a choice?

But I must be open. Loosen the bowel of my spirit and observe whatever drops on to the shelf. What do I see? Submission to the will of women. Uncoerced? Maybe so. Unconscious activity which enforces the power of women who I allow to dominate. Also my mother.

I think Michaelis has assessed me to be homosexualistic, all his constructions on this fairy foundation laid. So his building topples. But I am living in the rubble. The dust I cough. Like bitter ashes – why should I eat?

Take another line of direction. Leave behind the stupidities of this Michaelis. To Laura I gave a present. A present and a past. Maybe a future. Even if it has cost me everything, even if she with the garbage throws it out. Now she has some pontoon in the sea of herself. A pontoon made from the debris of my ruination.

They are like the sea, you know this? Moving and shifting. They cannot be controlled. You cannot predict them. Nor on them can you build anything. Always to be with them, to join them, you must tread water, dive, swim, and when on your back you turn to float and relax a bigger wave comes to break on your face and choke the breath. Women.

And the sex-change – Bruce/Daisy – wants to become this. How can you change the land into the sea? The sea into the land maybe, like the silted harbour at Ephesus.

Even after the damage has been done, the tidal wave having torn the village from the shore, the dead children tossed in mud, she had the gall to apologise, to thank me, as, after a storm, you have a glassy calm in the bay. A stillness which denies all the rage and damage and brutish power which the night before was keeping you from sleep.

They are uncontainable. Even in her wheelchair, in the autumn of herself, my mother is irrepressible. And always I am drawn, the swimmer on the high cliff, skin parched by Apollo, making his dive.

I try to make a balance of account. Not for money.
Money is not the problem. Next year maybe I have my
own film development fund, a fund made from the healing
of damaged people (also from the cleansing of promiscuous
bowels). For projects to be shot in Greece. Bring the
money here. More power with the authorities. Then on
to the island council. Subsidise the farming. Finish the
tourism. Make old Greece again, the Institut the only
place on the island where foreigners can come. And the
institut guests will subsidise the island so that the
peasants can be peasants, not selling Coca-Cola to Danish
computer engineers and playing Bob Marley tapes all day.
My kingdom.
Dream on.
No. My balance of account is moral/existential. Now I
start to understand that the cost of liberating one soul can
indeed be very great. The salvation may not necessarily be
permanent and the cost may be too great. Yet, this path
have I chosen.
Sometimes, the plumber of the soul, when he unblocks
the pipe which has jammed the whole system, he is
drenched in the shit of many others. So. Take a shower.
Move on.
Easy to say.
And yet.
And yet, who will after me look? Who will take my head
and lay it upon her breast and to me say, there, there,
darling, don't be sad, do not frightened be. Who will look
after me now that Maria is dead? Who?
My chance for that is gone. For peace I had hoped. Now
the suspension of chaos, day by day, hour by hour, is the
best to which I can look forward.
At first, when Maria disappeared, I thought to myself, we
have argued; she is angry with me, but she will recover from
this. She knew before then, surely, of my photography, my

monitors, the cameras in the rooms concealed. All part of the therapeutic process.

But the zoom trained upon her house in the valley? The time-phased photographs?

An extension of my vigilance. Nothing more.

She did not see it that way.

She broke the coded lock on my tower door. This was an aggression; a treachery. I am violated, no less than if she made an entry into my skull with a power drill. No one knows that she came to the tower on the night of her disappearance. No one but Laura.

Maria strolled into a struggle she did not understand. A struggle I have lost. Not a new conflict, perhaps, but the old conflict played out again with new actors, leading to the same nemesis. Mammi, Helga and now Laura. Will I always lose? Will I never learn?

In spite of my defeat, there is wind and sunshine, the sound of water on rock. No. These things have been polluted.

The night of her disappearance, I was in the tower, developing a roll of zoom pictures. I could not find the shower pictures. Must be another roll, I was thinking. Still in the camera—

I hear a banging, think another shutter has from the hinge come loose in the wind. Then the darkroom door swings open, bringing white light, destroying some of the pictures. A bad omen.

Violation. This was our theme. Mine and Maria's.

Was mine of her or hers of me the greater? Even I could see, my case was weak.

Dolt!

Down on your knees you should have dropped, begged forgiveness, at whatever cost. From the training manual the first rule you abandoned: always validate the feelings of the subject; establish trust before you show the subject her feelings in a new light.

Surviving pictures she saw. Enough to know my habits. She ran from the tower, down the spiral stairs, out into the night.

After a day – not an easy one, attending to patients, running groups, securing the tower – I sent the kitchen boy to her house in the valley.

Empty.

I sent him to the village. The port. The shipping office. To ask.

Nothing.

Michaelis in London I telephoned. You know what he said. The heart of the man is frozen like a fish-finger.

They found her body on the rocks. Both her legs were broken. Her lungs had a little water in them. Her skull was fractured. Five of her ribs were broken, as was her left wrist. Her spleen was ruptured. But her face was perfect still. The coroner calculated the time of her death. The night of our argument. About two hours after we had parted.

The polizei telephoned, thanks be to God, rather than arrive straight away at my place. I had time to clean up the tower before they came to look. All my Maria pictures, all my naked girls and boys to ashes turned. I check the zoom. Empty of film. But I was sure I had left the roll with the girls playing in the shower. In a heightened state of feeling I had been. Who knows?

One or two shots I had to keep. OK. OK. These I posted to myself along with the tapes from the monitor cameras.

Polizei all over the Institut. Frightening the clients. Dario, he had a seizure from fear. Helicopter to Siros. We charge a mark-up. I made a contribution to the benevolent fund of polices.

Later, when it was calmer, I fast-forwarded through the tape from the monitor watching Maria's room in the Institut. Can you believe the tape runs out even before she came to the tower? I will never know. Not for sure.

Papers to fill. A coroner's hearing to attend in Siros.

Emergency replacements flown in from Florida. A funeral in Athens. Expensive in time and money.

She is gone. I am all alone.

She was beautiful. She was good. Why?

Why? It cannot be that my vigilance, guardian over all her actions, all her days, would drive her to this. I was watching over her. To protect. To keep safe from harm. Can you not understand?

I drove her to it? you say. What do you know?

Everywhere my profession is invaded by amateurs and halfwits, mountebanks (yes, I looked it up in the dictionary) and impostors. You have no grounds for this belief.

None.

How could she have fallen? She knew the paths too well. Sure-footed like an island goat.

So, you see, there is not even the sound of water on rock, nor even the sound of the wind to console me. These things have joined the IRS, the proponents of new German cinema, Helga, my mother and my father. They abide with the enemy.

And I?

A finished thing of the bald head and the broken hopes. A plump one with a fat tax bill to pay.

And this was not yet the worst. Two nights after the funeral in Athens, I am in my tower of full elevation, watching the monitor for the room of Laura. She rises from the bed where she had been reading a book—

—leaves my view—

—returns into the frame holding a packet. She stands before the camera, close, looking straight at the lens which is concealed in the ceiling.

'Are you there, Herr Institut Direktor? I'm sure you are. My ever-watchful one.'

She opens the packet.

'I had these developed in the village. Do you want to see them?'

She shuffles the pictures.

'Now, before you get excited, I want you to know that I had copies made, a second set, and I've put them somewhere very safe. Here's a good one.'

Up to the camera she holds a shot from my zoom: Maria drying Laura on the terrace with a white towel. A beautiful shot: good composition; sharp focus; the camouflage of almond-leaf shadow upon the skins of both women.

For the first time since they found Maria, I did weep. Not sobs – they later came – but water from the eyes, salt taste on my lips, throat tight with loss.

'And here's another.' The pictures now I cannot so clearly see. Four more photos she shows to the camera. 'Let's save the rest for another night, shall we?'

The roll from the zoom lens.

'Up there in your tower.' She sits upon the bed. 'I can see the attraction. The wonderful views. And such technology! Like *Thunderbirds*. You must feel safer now the locks are fixed. But – as you taught me – we shouldn't always trust our feelings, should we?'

She takes off her skirt.

'You taught me to objectify my feelings, look at them from a new angle. That's just what I want you to do, Herr Direktor.'

And then the panties and the shirt and the bra.

'I shaved my legs. Look!'

Like the sea. You should fear water. Water, fire and glass. Those three you must always beware. Mammi, Helga, Laura.

'One day, Franzie, all this will be mine. If I want it. Tomorrow, maybe. Or next year. Whenever I like. But until then I want you to be a busy director and I'll be your busy assistant, and we'll put all the humpty-dumpties together again.

'Except Maria.' Laura sits on the ground and holds her knees. 'She can't be put back together again, can she?

'Did you look at her body, Franz? Have you seen what we did to her? She couldn't fly like you or me.'

Ah, Laura, you know too much.

'She wasn't strong enough for this, Franz. You should never have brought her here.'

Now that Laura is weeping I wish that I could be in the room with her. To comfort, you understand. And to be comforted.

'Not strong enough for a pair of old frauds like you and me,' Laura said. And then she muttered something else, but the microphone could not pick it up.

The loss of Maria and the liberation of Laura were not the only issues with which I was concerned. It was the tough time. Late July, always with a big influx of guests. I bring in extra potentiators from Florida, also one of Michaelis's pupils from London.

There was a triumph of failure in me – can you understand? I could not throw Laura from my Institut, so I was forced to make the sacrifice of my peace of mind at the altar of her recovery a self-evident good.

Thank you.

But would she reciprocate the generosity? Still the photos she had, still the knowledge of my tower, the videos, the notes, the pictures.

You must take a bodily equivalent to understand this invasion. An angry child, inside my skull squatting, tapping at the inside of my head with a sharp spear. This was my penance.

We professionals call this a negative symbiosis. In this there is trauma but also comfort, companionship, even intimacy. Together we would grieve. But always through the camera in the ceiling of her room. Never more together than that. Never face to face.

I should have gone to London. Done a counter-transference session with Michaelis. Maybe given Michaelis a piece of my

mind. But it was not possible. The enema boys came
thick and fast from Mykonos. The word of mouth for
my Institut grew year by year on the island of Sodom.
We must service their needs. The hydrology room broke
down and the man from Athens took two days to arrive
and three days to fix up the bastard machine. Even German
plumbing sometimes it fails.

I reject Michaelis's self-determining choice theorem. How
could it be that into this mayhem – Euroqueens queuing for
a broken irrigation machine, Laura with a gun to my head
(inside, pointing the gun) and even the Boston alcoholic
couple making trouble over the fees (medical insurers
refusing to pay for any further treatment) – in this stew
of dysfunction I have chosen to drown?

Pah!

Laura was changed – becalmed – but her calm, of course,
I could not trust. I was in a bad way: arrhythmic, sweat
glands too open, the smell of my perspiration all wrong, my
body odour tainted by the toxins of grief. The osteopath was
making daily crunches on my spine, shifting the plates of my
skull. Also, I had a touch of peripheral neritis, a twitching
beside the left eye.

Who plans these humiliations? You still think I chose,
Michaelis?

I tried to meditate but my thoughts whirled and wheeled
like a flock of migrating birds, Laura soaring amongst them,
wheeling, preparing for a departure but refusing to leave.

19

No, they do not always heal. I admit it.

We must open the wound wider, suck out the poison. When we explore the wound they feel as if they are being healed, but this is an illusion. Growth is not always a healing process. Sometimes a greater wound you must inflict.

This I should know, the summer I have had. Blow upon blow and no shelter. Alas, poor Franz. You cannot see it but the tears splash upon the keyboard. Not for myself do I weep. Believe it!

The women – without Maria, how could I hope to understand them? Laura was now my newly self-elected assistant. I was an exile in my own kingdom, dealing only with the men. Watching. Watching.

Laura wore the look, now, of someone who knows how to be looked at. The pleasure of watching her changed. No longer the secret avid gaze upon the unknowing innocent.

He must have experienced this when out of the garden He slung our forebears.

Laura sat in her room, talking to the camera. Whispering to me.

To watch the house of Maria brings only grief.

Maria opened a wound in Laura and out came the monsters. And into my wound still Laura digs her spear.

With the photographs, sure, but with her knowledge of the tower, she had disrobed me of my authority. The focus of the Institut day became not my morning group but Laura's sunset ritual:

Up on the terrace, on a level with my turret in the tower of full elevation. I watch them gather: the Floridian potentiators, Amanda (pill-head), Constantine (depressive), Giannina (food problem), Arnold (therapy tourist), Thérèse (sex addiction), and the rest. Even some passing trade from the colonics.

They gather in a circle around the enlightened one. On cushions under the palm tree, with ashtrays and a bowl of fruit which she passes to them, like some benevolent priestess.

At seven o'clock, when they are all there, she calls out to me.

'Herr Direktor, come join us. We need you.'

I descend from the tower and lock the door. I walk past the dining room and out into the golden light of the terrace. She leads them in applause, the mockery a collusion between the two of us alone. There is always a cushion on her right. My cushion. And on her left, a cushion upon which no man nor woman may sit.

She always begins with the same words:

'On my right sits the man who will set you free. But you must trust the process. On my left is a place where Maria used to sit.'

There are some moments of silence for Maria.

'Let us take her memory as a token of all we have lost. So, on my right sits my father, living but lost to me. And on my left, my sister, dead but never lost.'

Then my unpaid potentiator, my familiar, my heir, pours out her confession, tempting the others to open in her wake.

'My name is Laura. My father is called John Blade. I used to call him my weekend father. On Friday evenings my twin sister Lizzie and I were driven to London by our mother. We knew all the landmarks. Passing the airport, where the trains run alongside the road, we hoped to be caught in the shadow of a take-off. A bridge at the top of a hill rested on V-shaped stanchions. The buses began to be red near the place where they sold caravans next to a railway station. Then there was a *Jesus Saves* poster peeling on the side of a church, and the common with its empty fields and stunted trees. Buses clogged every street. We waited for them to cross the bridge in front of us. We saw houseboats, flour mills and men working in a big gap between houses. Mummy told us they were building tower blocks.

'When Mummy pressed a button next to a door Daddy's voice would come out of a grille below the button. We took turns shouting – It's Lizzie and Laura – then the door would open. Mummy put us in the lift with our suitcase. When we reached the top Daddy was there with Margaret and it was the weekend. Margaret had been our nanny; one day Mummy told us that she had gone away. Then Daddy went away. When we saw him again we were happy because he had found Margaret. He said he was looking after her for us. She looked prettier, more grown-up in the dresses Daddy bought for her.

'His flat was high up on the sixth floor. We played on a balcony which looked out over the city. We pretended we were sailors in the crow's nest. Mummy never mentioned Margaret and Margaret never mentioned Mummy.

'Before bedtime on Saturdays Daddy sat me on his lap and read to me from a book that I did not understand. I loved the smell of his clothes, his scratchy chin and the vibrations of his voice against my cheek. When Margaret put us to bed we ate the chocolate that Mummy always gave us.

'When we were at boarding school, Daddy took us out every third weekend. His car was bigger than Mummy's and we preferred those weekends. We collected Margaret from the local pub and went to a restaurant for lunch. Daddy let us drink wine. He bought us presents: books for Lizzie and paints for me. Lizzie and I had two of everything we wanted. The girls in my dorm were jealous until Julia and Mary Reed came to the school and they had two of everything as well. They told the others it was better to have one family and one of everything than two and two of everything. It did not make much sense to me.

'I had two big sets of colouring pencils, made in Switzerland. Joy Fairweather did not have any colours so I gave her one of my sets. The others were angry. The head told me that I was right to be generous but wrong to give things away unless I could give the same amount to everyone. That was when I realised that teachers can be wrong. I told everyone they could use my colours but only Joy Fairweather used them.

'When I was thirteen I was allowed to take the train to London with Lizzie. We passed the place where they sold caravans by the railway station; it looked quite different from the train. We had a way of working out the arrival platform from the track we took across the river. Lizzie opened the door to Daddy's flat with her own set of keys. No sign of Daddy or Margaret. Lizzie said it was more fun when they were away. I looked out at the dirty city below us; houses with grand white fronts had blackened metal steps running up their backs. Cars and garbage filled the mews where Mummy left us on Friday nights.

'Lizzie invited friends over. They drank Daddy's whisky. I took the television to bed with me and watched an old film in which people kept their promises. After that I went for weekends at Joy Fairweather's.

'As I said, I am Laura. People took to calling me Lorry when I was eighteen. I didn't mind being fat. It's better than not eating and ending up in hospital like Lizzie did.

'One day Daddy and I went to Oxford to look at my paintings in a gallery attached to one of the colleges. As we drove back along the motorway everything felt balanced, calm, almost perfect. We passed teddy-bear clouds and corn-bright squares darned into the valleys. Daddy drove fast with the radio on. We saw ribbons of new housing, a chrome turret like a church spire and a glider coming in to land over the road in front of us. From up there the motorway must look like a gash through the bed of green, an ant-track through the jungle.

'Daddy wanted to help me sell my paintings. I told him I could travel without a nepotist ticket. I was sorry as soon as I said it. We were silent all the way back to London. He stopped in my street and waited for me to get out. Didn't say goodbye. There was a telephone engineer kneeling before one of those green boxes on the pavement. He opened it up with a stubby key and there were all the wires tying everyone to everyone else. So many wires: red and green; blue and black; yellow and orange. They were bunched like the stems of flowers. With so many wires it must be hard to make the right connections. If one of the engineers were to spin off and forget himself it would all fall to pieces. I had an urge to tempt him, to say, Come now, my man, isn't it time we simplified things?, and pull out a bunch or two. He wore a headset which he plugged into the green box. I thought of all the anonymous callers, cold-sellers, wrong numbers and crossed lines.

'Mummy has always been plump and has learnt to carry her weight with dignity. She avoids trousers and anything tight. I had her example to follow. She wrote me letters explaining on the back that she couldn't afford the stamp because "your father" was late with the alimony again. I sent her a book of stamps once but she gave it to the daily. She did not want my charity.

'Men used to keep away from me. The ones who persisted found themselves modelling for my paintings. I made them stand with their arms in the air like goalkeepers. They soon went away. I was pledged to self-sufficiency. Other people broke my rhythm. Until Billy.'

*   *   *

Listening to Laura's ramblings seemed to open up the other patients. What can I do? Sometimes there is a narrative. Sometimes it is the father who in London lived. Sometimes the mother. She always changes elements of the story around, delving for something which the mere rearranging of the parts will not reveal. The facts may not always be correct, but there is a truth in what she makes the reorganised facts express.

She preaches my body-awareness, my stool chart, gives praise to the plumber of the soul.

How can I complain? Pretty much the queen of the fair she has become.

Another evening, as she began her story—

'Once upon a time, I took a trip to New York. Or rather my friend Billy asked me along, as you might ask along a roommate you cannot shrug off, out of pity—'

—I realised that I was happy, wrapped in the coils of a blanket which for so long I had refused, from which – try as I might – I could never release myself.